Legends, Stories and Ghostly Tales of Abingdon and Washington County, Virginia

By Donna Akers Warmuth

Other books by Donna Akers Warmuth

Plumb Full of History A Story of Abingdon, Virginia (High Country Publishers)

Abingdon, Virginia: Images of America (Arcadia Publishing)

Boone, North Carolina: Images of America (Arcadia Publishing)

Blowing Rock, North Carolina: Images of America (Arcadia Publishing)

Cover design: Beth Jacquot

ISBN 1-59513-006-3
Copyright 2005 by Donna Akers Warmuth
Printed in the United States of America
All Rights Reserved

Laurel Publishing
410 Parkcrest Drive
Boone, North Carolina 28607

*To my Akers family and my husband, Greg,
and our two sons, Owen and Riley*

*Thank you from the bottom of my heart for
your support and belief in me.*

Table of Contents

Acknowledgments

I would like to thank the many people who provided me with ghost stories, legends, and assistance with research for this book. I would like especially to thank Gary and Marie Frank, owners of 153 West Booksellers & Gallery in Abingdon for providing support and belief in my ability to put together this collection, in spite of a difficult pregnancy and a subsequent "easy" baby. I appreciate the help, assistance and support of Melissa Watson, Kitty Henninger, John Gregory, Gene Mathis, Joella Barbour, Carmen Blevins, and the other helpful staff and volunteers at the Historical Society of Washington County, Virginia. The society's library and archives, located in the historic train station on Depot Square, are an incredible resource for historical information.

The ghost tour of the Martha Washington Inn that Pete Sheffey, veteran employee and Master of Spirits, conducted for me was eerie, entertaining, and fascinating. I would highly recommend all visitors to Abingdon join Mr. Sheffey on one of his ghost tours of the Martha Washington Inn. He's a gentleman full of stories and charm, and I hope he will write his own book someday. Thanks for kindly allowing me to include your stories.

I appreciate the assistance of the following persons who provided me with stories for this collection: Brandon Aird, L.C. Angle, Pat Brown, Vivian Coletti, Lou Crabtree, Phebe Cress, Donna Cruise, Jennifer DeHart, Shannon Gregory, Mary Lou Frazier Harrington, G. Lee Hearl, Helen Henley, B.B. Huff, Dave and Jo Johnson, Johnston Memorial Hospital staff, Dan Leidig, Glenn Litton, Bud Phillips, Cynthia Salyers, Rob Salyers, Carol Schwartz, Glenn Sexton, Diane Silver, Katie Sykes, Robert Vejnar, Robert Weisfeld, Eleanor Williams, and Jason Willis.

Thanks to the wonderful editing skills, confidence and encouragement of Diane Graham.

Finally, thank you for the limitless support of my Akers family and husband, Greg, and children, Owen and Riley. This book would not have been possible to write without the belief, assistance, and support of my family, friends, and faithful readers.

Introduction

Every culture in the world has passed down stories and legends. These stories serve to identify the group, to inspire, and to develop a deep love of family and the land itself. We are fortunate because the isolation of the Appalachian region has fostered a rich collection of stories, legends, ghost stories, and myths. In southwest Virginia, the mixture of various ethnic backgrounds including Irish, Scot, English, Welsh, German, Swiss, and French, has created a varied folklore tradition that adapted to the challenges of this first western frontier.

The ghost stories, oral histories and legends have helped to make the southern Appalachian people distinctive and who we are today. Before radio, television, and movies, the telling of stories was the primary means of entertainment. For instance, if you stop in a small country store in Brumley Gap, you are sure to find some older men sitting around and sharing stories. The ghost stories and legends of Abingdon and surrounding Washington County are very real to the people here and serve as reminders of the rich history and heritage of the past.

A legend is defined as a traditional prose narrative, set in this world, in the past, involving human characters, which the teller and audience regard as fact (Barden 1991:2). However, one can tell an unbelievable legend, merely for the enjoyment of the story. The question of whether the story or legend is true is not important, for the stories take on their own life and provide information about the culture, the region, the land, and beliefs.

One can find categories of common legends, including hidden treasure, the supernatural, place-name stories, and legendary people. While I found stories in these categories, I also discovered more distinctive southwest Virginia themes about Indians, Civil War conflict, and frontier heroes. Legends often have the purpose of imparting a moral lesson, such as the dangers of being involved in witchcraft and being respectful of graveyards.

The South and indeed Appalachia seem to have more than their fair share of ghosts. Washington County and Abingdon are no exception. Generations have told these ghost stories and legends to their children and their children's children. The stories in this collection are not documented by scholarly research, and many are not mentioned in local history books. However, the stories, and the buildings, or the memories of these buildings, that they are often associated with, have lasted through the years.

Obviously, documentation of ghost stories is a difficult business. However, credible witnesses have documented many of these stories through the years. Doubters may say rational explanations exist for apparitions of pale children and the sounds of muffled footsteps. But, one wonders if these things are simply beyond our human understanding and that a psychic world exists that is separate from our world.

Guided ghost tours in Abingdon can provide a first-hand account of stories and legends. Pete Sheffey, long-time employee of the Martha Washington, can claim to know all of the ghost stories of the illustrious "Martha." His grandfather and father were longtime employees at the Inn, so the Sheffey family's oral history contains many of these stories. Contact the Martha Washington Inn for information on booking a tour by Mr. Sheffey, for it will be a memorable experience. Also, Donna Marie Emmert is the acclaimed "Haint Mistress" of Abingdon and provides chilling ghost tours through downtown, supplemented with a healthy dosing of local history.

I hope this collection will cause you to remember and retell these ghost stories, legends and historical tales. I also hope these stories can rekindle your own memories and encourage you to tell your children and grandchildren your own family stories. This process keeps the Appalachian legends and oral histories alive and part of our family and culture. These stories are still here, although they may be hidden like a cache of Civil War gold, and they need to be told and remembered.

Please note: by writing these stories, the author is not taking a stance either for or against the question of whether ghosts exist. Rather, the purpose of this collection is to entertain and educate the audience, by collecting, researching and recording this assemblage of tales of southwest Virginia. You, the reader, must decide if these spirits and stories are real.

Also, please respect the privacy of the residents of homes mentioned in this book and do not intrude on them. Only in Colonial Williamsburg, are all homes open for tours.

If you do become frightened or uneasy after reading these, you may follow this simple "spell" to ward off ghosts and other evil spirits:

Place a pair of well-worn shoes just inside the main entry into your home.

The evil spirits will believe that the owner of the house is standing guard just inside the house, and they will not enter.

Ch. 1 Summary History of Abingdon and Washington County

By the time the first settlers entered southwest Virginia, they found only traces of a previous Native American occupation. Even today, the abundance of points (arrowheads), pieces of pottery, and stone chips from knapping (flaking stones to make a tool) found in the area bear witness to the first occupants of the Holston River valley. At the time of European settlement, this fertile river valley was a hunting grounds of the Cherokee, Shawnee and other tribes. The Native Americans called the Holston River, the main tributary of the valley, "Hogohegee." The earliest surveys refer to the tributary as the Indian River.

Thomas Walker and surveyors from the Loyal Land Company first surveyed lands in the area in 1746. Washington County was formed in 1777 from Fincastle County (formed from Botetourt County) and named in honor of George Washington. Later, Scott, Russell, Wise, Dickenson, Buchanan, Tazewell, and Smyth counties would be formed from the larger Washington County.

Early pioneers were coming in search of inexpensive land, wealth, game and personal freedom. Abingdon is one of southwest Virginia's earliest towns and later became a gateway to the West. In 1760, Daniel Boone provided the first name for the settlement, "Wolf Hills," due to an incident in which wolves from the underground caves attacked his hunting dogs. The first houses were built about 1768, and Dr. Thomas Walker donated 120 acres of land on which to build a town. The settlement became known as "Black's Fort" for the fort built in 1776 by Joseph Black for protection from the Native Americans.

In 1778, the town was named Abingdon to honor Martha Washington's ancestral parish in England. Because of its strategic location of the Wilderness Road leading into Kentucky and the unexplored west, the town of Abingdon became a stopping point for travelers. In 1793, the first post office in southwest Virginia was established in Abingdon, and the government distributed mail from here to the rest of southwestern Virginia, east Tennessee and Kentucky.

In 1835, Martin's *Gazetteer of Virginia* described the town as follows: 150-200 dwelling houses (many brick), an academy for females, an academy for males, two hotels, three taverns for wagoners, one manufacturing flour mill, nine mercantile houses, three groceries, one woolen and two cotton manufactories, four tanyards with saddle and harness manufactories, ten blacksmith shops, one hat manufactory and store, six wheelwrights and wagon makers, two cabinet warehouses, and two boot and shoe manufactories.

The town can boast three governors of Virginia as natives: David Campbell, John B. Floyd Jr. and Wyndham Robertson, as well as key statesmen and judges. Another claim to fame for the town is the Barter Theatre, the state theatre of Virginia, known for its professional theatre productions. The Civil War was a turbulent time for the town, because of two Union raids. A bitter Union soldier burned the courthouse and several other historic buildings as Stoneman's Union forces left the town. After the war the town's economy rebounded, and the railroad and lumbering industries helped develop the area in the early 1900s (Summers 1989:1-30).

Today, Abingdon has carefully preserved the architecture and ambience of its early history. Washington County contains many historic resources and has a rich agricultural history all its own. Tourism and a service economy have sustained a healthy economic environment for the residents and businesses. The economy is changing from an agricultural and manufacturing focus to a technology, education, tourism, and service base.

Martha Washington College c. 1880
(Courtesy of Historical Society of Washington County, Virginia)

Ch. 2 Spirited Martha Washington Inn

How many historic inns can boast four stars and twice as many ghosts? Only the Martha Washington Inn in Abingdon seems to have this claim to fame. From Civil War soldiers to mysterious college girls in long dresses, the spirits are as numerous as today's guests in this lovely Federal-style hotel.

There are many stories of chilling encounters, between employees, guests and the spirit world. Some guests and employees have seen young students from the Martha Washington College and wounded Confederate soldiers. The inn's staff and guests tell of other eerie happenings, such as cold spots in hallways, doorknobs turning on their own, and apparitions seen in the hallways.

The Master of the Martha's ghosts is Pete Sheffey, who has a 40-some year history at the Martha Washington Inn, as bellman and concierge. His father and grandfather both were bellmen at the inn.

Mr. Sheffey is gregarious and provides fascinating historical and ghost tours of the Inn. He took me on a "private" ghost tour that sent shivers down to my toes.

To understand the context of the ghosts, one must understand the building's history. The red brick grand dame has seen the growth of the frontier town and its rebirth into an antique and arts center. The Federal style center section of the hotel dates back to 1832, when built as a private home for General Francis Preston and his wife Sarah Buchanan Campbell Preston. The Prestons made their fortune from the salt mines in nearby Saltville. The house was considered a mansion even in those early times.

Francis Preston studied law and was a graduate of William & Mary College. He later served in Congress from 1793 to 1797 and also in the General Assembly. Sarah Buchanan Campbell Preston also had an impressive pedigree. She was the daughter of General William Campbell, who led the Washington County soldiers at the Battle of King's Mountain, and Elizabeth Henry, a sister to Patrick Henry.

After 1858, the Preston house became Martha Washington College, an exclusive girls' school. After the school closed, the inn passed through several owners, and today, it has been carefully restored and refurbished with antiques. The building is a Historical Hotel of America and is listed on the National Register of Historic Places.

Yankee Sweetheart

The Civil War was a traumatic time in southwest Virginia, with several Union raids, and food and supply shortages for residents. It's not surprising that several stories from that time live on through legends at the Martha Washington Inn. The most common ghost story told about the Inn concerns a tragic love affair between a student at Martha Washington College and her Yankee sweetheart. Although still a girls' college, Martha Washington College served as a hospital during the Civil War. Several of the girls didn't return home during the war but bravely volunteered to stay at the school as nurses. Captain John Stoves, a Yankee officer, was severely wounded and captured in town. Soldiers carried Capt. Stoves through the cave system under Abingdon and up a secret stairway to the third floor of the building. Captain Stoves lay gravely wounded in what is now Room 403. For weeks, a young student named Beth nursed and cared for him. She found herself falling in love with the brave captain, and he returned her sentiments. Often, Beth would lovingly play the violin to ease his pain and suffering. But, their love was not to last for long. As he lay dying, he called, "Play something, Beth, I'm going."

Unfortunately, Beth was too late to escort him out with a song, because he died suddenly. Beth tearfully played a sweet southern melody as a tribute to him. When a Confederate officer entered and explained that he was taking Captain Stoves as a prisoner, Beth faced him triumphantly and said, "He has been pardoned by an officer higher than General Lee. Captain Stoves is dead." Beth died a few weeks later from typhoid fever.

Many of the female students who later attended the college, as well as inn employees and guests, have heard Beth's sweet violin music in the night. Others report that Beth visits Room 403 to comfort her Yankee soldier (Curtis 1928: 146-148).

The building's use as a girls' college is a fascinating part of its history. The Holston Conference of the United Methodist Church acquired the building in 1858 and established Martha Washington College, an exclusive women's college. The college was one of the earliest in southwestern Virginia. The community was a major supporter of the college and held fairs to benefit the school. The college welcomed local ladies and women from all over the East Coast as students from 1860 until 1919. The school could accommodate as many as 150 boarding students. Later, the campus included four brick buildings, which were heated by steam and lighted with incandescent electric lighting. After that, the building became part of Emory and Henry College, in nearby Emory. The college was closed in 1932 and stood empty for several years (Curtis 1928; King 1996:34).

Reappearing Bloodstain
A young Confederate soldier in Abingdon was assigned to carry

important papers about the location of the Union army to General Robert E. Lee. He was hopelessly in love with a young woman at the college. Knowing the risks he was facing, the brave soldier felt he must say farewell to his lady love before leaving. The soldier traveled through the cave system underlying Abingdon and used a secret stairway to enter the college. As the soldier was saying goodbye to his love, two Union officers came up the stairs and found them. With no way to escape, the young Confederate soldier was shot in front of his sweetheart, and, when he fell, his blood stained the floor. The strange thing is that through the years, the bloodstain continues to appear. Carpets over the area often develop mysterious holes over the stains. Even after the floors have been refinished, the stain continues to reappear, a sad reminder of the tragedy of the Civil War (Curtis 1928:148-150).

Galloping Ghost

Another story from Civil War times concerns a ghostly horse roaming through the grounds. On moonlit nights, many have seen a ghostly horse galloping around the grounds of the inn that simply disappears. One explanation is that the horse belonged to James Wyatt, the Yankee soldier who burned the courthouse and other buildings during Stoneman's 1864 raid through the town. Some accounts of the story report that after Wyatt was shot from his horse, the poor frightened animal ran to the grounds of Martha Washington College and galloped wildly around. It could be that the horse still searches for his long-gone master. Be careful if you should take a late night stroll through the beautiful grounds of the hotel (Curtis 1928:154-156).

Basement Moans

You could say the Martha has ghosts from top to bottom, including the basement. Another ghost story is that spirits of African American slaves haunt the basement. Previous owners may have kept the slaves in an underground chamber as punishment. Also, some of the slaves were rumored to have been buried within the walls of the basement, so their souls have simply stayed there. Staff members have heard strange noises and seen apparitions in the dark basement area (Sheffey, 2003).

Spirits of the Inn

The important role of the Inn during the Civil War and its use as a hospital during that time have left other unquiet spirits in the hallways. Both guests and staff have seen pale soldiers strolling the hallways and sitting in the lobby. This story comes from Pete Sheffey and was told to him by his grandfather. Wiley Sheffey, Pete's grandfather, also worked at the Martha Washington Inn. In 1937, Wiley had a strange encounter as he was on his 2 am round. Sheffey was walking down a dimly lit hallway, when he noticed a dark shape in the hallway. As he approached it, something reached out and touched him. Believing this to be a guest, Sheffey asked, "Can I help you?" He heard a moaned, "Help me." Sheffey saw that it was a man with part of his leg missing, apparently from a gunshot.

Thinking he might be a guest, Sheffey rushed downstairs and told the desk clerk. The desk clerk accompanied him to look in the hallway. They both saw a man in a gray uniform staggering down the hall. The desk clerk, not believing his eyes, called out, "What's wrong? The war's over." As the soldier leaned against the wall and took his sword out, the desk clerk fainted.

Then, Sheffey and the staff called the police to investigate the situation. The policeman saw a man crawling on the hallway, and he pulled his gun. The pale soldier struggled to pull his sword out. The policeman was shaking in his shoes and said, "Don't hurt me." The soldier dragged himself to the fire escape and managed to make his way down. Later, Sheffey and the desk clerk noticed bloodstains left on the fire escape. It took several cleanings before the blood could be washed off. Several guests have reported seeing a headless Confederate soldier limping along with a crutch, who simply disappears around a corner.

In a similar event, a lady staying at the Inn told Pete Sheffey one morning that she had enjoyed seeing the confederate reenactors in the inn last night. Mr. Sheffey raised his eyebrows and said, "Ma'am, there were no reenactors here last night." Mr. Sheffey believes the guest saw some of the soldiers' ghosts who frequent the inn. Other employees have seen a confederate soldier enter through the front door and walk down the hallway, and then disappear (Sheffey, 2003).

Some areas of the historic building seem to harbor more spirits than other areas. Pete Sheffey tells this story about an encounter with an "odd couple." One Sunday night at about 11 p.m., Pete Sheffey and the bellman were relaxing and talking in the hallway near the gift shop. The building was very quiet, and the men could hear the floors creaking and popping, as often happens in older buildings. As they talked, a man and woman appeared at the top of the stairs to the bottom floor. The man wore a double-breasted suit, and the lady wore a long gown covered by a long black coat and a bonnet. The two men looked at each other, wondering about their strange clothing. Were they guests in the hotel? It was then that they noticed the couple was almost floating or gliding on the floor. Sheffey cleared his throat and asked, "Can we help you?"

The couple didn't answer but floated toward the doors into the ballroom, and then, they vanished. The men tried the doors to the ballroom, but they were locked. Sheffey and his friend told the security guard when he came on duty later about the strange couple. The group of three men walked around the hotel looking for signs of the ghostly couple. Suddenly, down another hallway, the three men saw the couple gliding along again. This time they felt cold air, and Sheffey remembers that he caught a musty smell, like something old. The couple turned and looked at the group. The woman held up her hand and beckoned, and they disappeared again. Were they trying to communicate with the living? Then, that night, as Pete was going to his car, he saw them descending the fire escape, only to vanish away into thin air. No explanations for this apparition have been found (Sheffey, 2003).

Certain rooms in the Inn are known to be haunted. In fact, some staff members refuse to enter these rooms and will avoid them at all costs. Pete Sheffey tells of a frightening encounter back in 1984 in

Room 210, the Virginia Suite. The section near Room 210 had been blocked off because of a Garden Club meeting. Pete was sent to check on a problem with a TV remote in Room 210. As he fit in his master key in the room door, he knocked and said, "Bellman," as was his custom, even though the room was vacant. He tried to push the door open, but it felt as if someone was holding it on the other side. Finally, he pushed again, and the door finally opened.

As Pete entered, he felt something pat him on the cheek. Pete turned the lights on in the room to see if anyone was in there. He suddenly felt a person right behind him, and this time he felt a pat on the back. But the room was unoccupied! Terrified, Pete tried to run away, but he found he couldn't move. Pete described it as if someone else was controlling his body. He managed to pick up the remote, but then he dropped it. Pete began backing away toward the door and he said the only thing he could think of that might help him. He said, "God loves you, Beth." Pete was able to barely get out the door before the door slammed in his face. Strangely, Beth was the name of the Martha Washington College student who played violin to her dead Yankee sweetheart (Sheffey, 2003).

The Napoleon Room, or Room 302, has its share of odd stories and strange encounters. The Napoleon Room is one of the grandest rooms in the Inn. An ornate bed which supposedly belonged to Napoleon graces the center of the room. The room is in the old Preston home section, the original building. Some speculate that the room was used as a morgue when the inn was a hospital during the Civil War. Upon entering the room, several visitors have felt a strange atmosphere. Guests of the inn and staff have seen people sitting in the chairs of the room, perhaps members of the wealthy Preston family. The spirits seem absorbed in their daily life and don't notice today's visitors. Others have seen students from the former Martha Washington College gliding through the room. The long graceful skirts of the students sway as they cross the room. Their girlish laughter has no sound (Sheffey, 2003).

Pete told a story of a couple staying at the inn in Room 302. Suddenly, from their deep sleep, they both were awakened by a strange feeling. A young girl of about 14 years, clad in a long dress, was standing at the foot of their bed. Thinking it was another guest, the woman asked, "Would you please leave the room?" The girl simply looked at them and then jerked the blankets off the couple. Then, she disappeared. As you can imagine, the couple had a restless night and checked out first thing the next morning (Sheffey, 2003). There are certain brave guests who will request to stay in the Napoleon Room, but many other regulars know to avoid the room.

Another area of the Inn with strange sightings is the front room on the third floor, also part of the original Preston house. At night, one guest saw a figure of a woman in a long dress in the suite. She turned the lights on in the room and heard a noise. She yelled, "Who's there?" The door to the next room slammed in her face. The guests in the room next door came out to see what was happening. They also saw a ghostly mist inside the room. Many guests have reported lights coming on in this particular room, even after being turned off (Sheffey, 2003).

Even after all these encounters, Pete Sheffey has remained on staff at the Martha. He doesn't feel threatened enough to leave but seems to view the spirits almost as old friends. The numerous spirits who still live here don't seem to mind sharing the space with the guests of the Inn.

Barter Theatre in 1940. (Courtesy of Historical Society of Washington County, Virginia)

Ch. 3 Various & Sundry Abingdon Ghosts

Because of Abingdon's long history, residents have passed down many ghost stories about buildings and sites throughout the town. These stories have changed and evolved through the years. Several published books have included the most popular ghost stories associated with buildings in town, such as the Barter Theatre, the Cave House, and the Tavern. In this section, I've summarized a few of these "tried and true" stories for old times sake, and included several previously unpublished ones. If ever someone would survey towns for number of ghosts, Abingdon is sure to rank highly, especially given its small "living" population.

Barter Theatre

Many visitors to the world-famous Barter Theatre have seen the spirit of the theatre's founder, Robert Porterfield, in the building. Actors, theatre staff, as well as visitors, have reported seeing Mr.

Robert Porterfield accepts barter for entry in this 1949 photo. (Courtesy of Susan Yates)

Porterfield in various locations inside the building. It seems that even in the afterlife, the man who contributed so much to making the Barter Theatre the success that it is today just can't seem to leave it.

In 1933, Robert Porterfield, a charming, enterprising young man from the region, established the Barter Theatre. He developed an idea to provide acting jobs for his unemployed friends from New York and a market for the local population's bountiful produce. The public would obtain a ticket to see a show at the theatre by bartering produce, homemade crafts, or even livestock. As the locals said, one could trade "ham for Hamlet." Many famous actors began their careers here, including Ernest Borgnine, Ned Beatty, Hume Cronyn, Gregory Peck and Patricia Neal. Porterfield's curtain line before each production was, "If you like us, talk about us. If you don't, just keep your mouth shut!"

The building which houses the world-famous Barter Theatre dates back to 1832, when it was built as a church for the Sinking Spring Presbyterian congregation. The building was also used as a Temperance Hall during Prohibition and later as the town offices and jail. Today, the red brick building is the home of the Barter Theatre, the state theatre of Virginia.

Porterfield's Legacy

The death of Robert Porterfield was traumatic for the theatre, but many folks believe he is still there. Porterfield had such a love and connection to the theatre, so it's not surprising that he has never left. During dress rehearsals, actors believe that seeing his ghost in his favorite balcony seat brings luck for a good show. Theatre staff and guests have seen Porterfield's spirit in many locations in the theatre. On opening nights of a performance, many folks have spotted Mr. Porterfield dressed in his white dinner jacket as he always did for opening night.

After renovations to the Barter a few years ago, several employees carried the large oil painting of Robert Porterfield around the theatre to show him all the changes. Fortunately, he was pleased. His presence inevitably brings with it a sense of peace and good will (Price 1993:29-35).

Wampus Cat Lurks in Barter Alley

A sinister spirit known as a Wampus cat has been sighted in the alley outside the theatre. The Wampus cat is a common legend among this region of the Appalachians. The strange beast looks like a cat, but it stands on two legs. A couple visiting Abingdon believe they saw a Wampus Cat in the alley next to the Barter Theatre one late night. The two were enjoying a late night stroll, when suddenly they heard a hissing noise. They peered into the alley and saw a cat-like creature with evil green eyes standing up on two feet. The animal hissed again, and then dropped back down to four feet and disappeared into the alley. Obviously, the couple didn't follow the strange animal, but decided to return to their hotel room very quickly (Price 1993: 33-35).

The Tavern

Hearing of its tasty fare, you might decide to partake of a leisurely meal at the Tavern, but you would be shocked at the company you keep—a fair number of spirits who also dwell in the building. Stories of spirits include: a tavern barmaid, eerie red lights, and ghosts of Civil War soldiers. To appreciate the numerous sightings in the building, one must consider the long, and sometimes illustrious, history of taverns.

In the past, taverns were important in any settlement, but they were particularly popular in Abingdon. In fact, Governor David Campbell in 1782 describes Abingdon as having a courthouse, a jail

The Tavern, built about 1788. (Courtesy Historical Society of Washington County, Virginia)

and three taverns. In 1785, Campbell noted the town had grown by one or two more log houses, a blacksmith shop and another tavern. Taverns were places for locals to meet and socialize and to pick up mail, and for travelers to get a meal and a bed for the night. In a town like Abingdon, with its location on the Wilderness Road leading into Kentucky and the unexplored western frontier, taverns served hunters, explorers, and the pioneers who were moving westward.

The only remaining Abingdon tavern, properly named the Tavern, is located on Main Street just down from the courthouse. It was built about 1788, making it one of the older buildings in town. The design of the Tavern has been preserved, with a stone clad first floor and a frame upper structure which was later covered with stucco. The Tavern has served many uses: a bank, general store, bakery, cabinet store, barber shop, home, post office, antique store, and a restaurant. According to legend, the building was also a Civil War hospital and the attic walls still contain pencilled-in numbers for the sick beds. Today, the Tavern leans into the old brick sidewalk, almost as if sheltering its secrets.

Since it has a long and varied history, residents, visitors, and staff tell many tales of supernatural sightings here. Tavern staff have seen tables mysteriously cleaned off by helpful, but unseen waiters. Restaurant staff have had unexplained encounters with bar glasses that mysteriously fall down from the shelves. Other stories tell of a mysterious red glow visible in an upstairs window after dark from outside the building.

Back in the old days, taverns had almost a "wild west" atmosphere, where justice was often distributed without benefit of the law. Historical accounts tell of boisterous activities along "courthouse hill," so the Tavern likely enjoyed a wild reputation. With the nearby location of the Washington County Courthouse, several taverns and later hotels, all sorts of folks—including lawyers, criminals, travelers, wagoners, hunters, salesmen, and residents—gathered and socialized. One story commonly told about the Tavern is about a tired drover who played cards downstairs late into the night. The drover kept winning until, finally, the other players accused him of cheating. As the drover left the Tavern through the back alley, the other card players murdered him and left his body lying there. His ghost is said to haunt the Tavern and may be the source of the mysterious light seen inside (Taylor 2001:416-421; Price 1993:1-6)

Ghostly News in the *Abingdon Virginian* Office

This narrow, brick building at 170 E. Main is said to house a newspaper editor who just won't leave his job—even after his death. The Greenway Brothers Building was built in 1878 by James C. Greenway, David C. Greenway, and Thomas

Greenway Brothers Building, built in 1878.

Preston Trigg. These gentlemen constructed this three-part building with a bank in the center unit and retail stores on either side. The Dispensary, which dispensed alcohol, also occupied the building. The offices for the *Abingdon, Virginian* newspaper have occupied the building for many years—what stories the walls could tell! This newspaper, published by Martha M. Weisfeld and Robert Weisfeld, is Washington County's oldest business. W.H. Lyon established the newspaper in 1841, and since his death, he has had difficulty relinquishing control of the publication.

In the 1980s, a construction crew was renovating the building for several months. One day, a worker saw a man in an old-fashioned three-piece suit appear at the top of the stairs. The dapper gentleman stared at the surprised worker and began descending the stairs. Spooked by the apparition, all of the construction crew fled the building. The owners had to beg the contractors to return and finish the job. Robert Weisfeld believes it was the spirit of W.H. Lyon, just checking to be sure all was well at his beloved enterprise (Weisfeld, 2004).

Cave House

It may look like a house from a fairy tale, but the Cave House has mysterious residents and incidents that don't fit its innocent appearance. Built in 1857 by Adam Hickman, this lovely Gothic Revival style house has been well-preserved and maintains much of its architectural integrity. Mr. Hickman was an early Abingdon entrepreneur who owned a tannery and saddle and harness manufacturing business. The name, the Cave House, is derived from the cave system underlying the building, with an opening enclosed in an outbuilding behind the house. The old story goes that in 1760, Daniel Boone and a hunting group camped nearby, and wolves hidden in the caves attacked their dogs. And so it was that Daniel Boone called this settlement Wolf Hills. Robert Porterfield's widow, Mary Dudley Porterfield, owns the building and leases it to the Cave House Craft Association.

Stories from the house include a scary experience for a young

Cave House, built in 1857

Ernest Borgnine, novice actor at the Barter Theatre, which caused him to run out of the building and to never return. Staff who work at the craft cooperative have heard strange sounds from upstairs like marbles rolling across the floor, a rocker rocking away, and furniture being moved across the floor. Nobody was upstairs at the time. Shannon Gregory, a previous employee there, remembers being alone in the building and hearing furniture upstairs being moved and strange bumping noises. Shannon didn't work there much longer after this experience.

Other staff members have smelled the faint scent of cooked food in the back rooms which may have been the kitchen. One employee was so spooked by the sounds that he "got his gun," but after seeing nothing to shoot, he swore to quit his job. But, later, he decided that since nothing had hurt him in the building, the intentions of these spirits were not evil (Price 1993:23-28; Gregory, 2004).

Haints on Bradley Street

Southern Living magazine could easily feature this lovely, two-story white frame house. However, according to the owners of the house, Michael and Helen Henley and their son Matt, peaceful southern liv-

Henley family's haunted house on Bradley Street.

ing isn't the case inside the house.

The Henley family has experienced strange occurrences in the house from the time they moved in. The Henleys sometimes feel as if someone is sitting beside them on the couch. An unexplainable smell of peanut butter accompanies this presence, as if she's snacking on peanut butter crackers. The family does feel like the ghost is a female. She seems to prefer the company of the men of the family. Sometimes, the television turns on by itself in the middle of the night, and it's always on a certain channel. Matt, the young son, was alone in the house once and kept hearing noises from the laundry room. After he went to investigate, Matt saw that several boxes full of Christmas decorations had been knocked down from the shelf. Matt returned the boxes to the shelves, only to hear a noise and find them on the floor again. Finally, Matt said out loud, "Okay, if you want them on the floor, I'll just leave them." Perhaps Matt appeased this spirit, because the boxes no longer fell down.

The Henley family has returned home to find framed pictures knocked off the wall and scattered throughout the foyer and up the stairs. One photograph that fell in the foyer was an old view of the

Martha Washington Inn that shows two dark shadows near the entrance. The family hasn't ever felt threatened by the presence. She seems to have been accepted as part of the Henley family.

It's possible the house next door may be haunted too. Helen once saw a young man in an older military uniform staring out the window of the house and up the street, almost as if he were waiting for someone to arrive. For some reason, tenants do not stay in the house very long, leading the Henleys to wonder if there is another ghost next door (Henley, 2004).

Ghostly Granny of Johnston Memorial Hospital

You might expect a hospital to house ghosts since many folks pass over within its walls and may leave lingering energy. The hospital in Abingdon is no exception. The Johnston Memorial Hospital is located in the middle of town just north of the Washington County Courthouse. In 1905, Dr. E.T. Brady established the first hospital at the same site, but it was later demolished. The center section of the existing hospital was built in 1919. Additions to the facility, state of the art technology, as well as excellent and dedicated staff and doctors, have made the hospital a regional leader for healthcare.

Many employees and staff members at the hospital have experi-

Johnston Memorial Hospital, built in 1919. (Courtesy Johnston Memorial Hospital)

enced strange sightings and occurrences. Perhaps these happenings are common in such a place where people experience strong emotions and others leave the world of the living. The most common shared story is the sighting of a small gray-haired lady looking into office doors and peering around corners. Several nurses have seen a woman walking around a hallway corner, but when someone follows to check on her no one is there. Another odd incident is that nurses have heard a baby's cry echoing through all sections of the hospital, not just the OB floor where one would expect such a sound. Spirits sometimes are trapped in the same locations where they died, so perhaps these ghosts are doomed to lurk inside the hospital.

Another ghostly happening occurred a few years ago after the untimely death of a fellow nurse. One night, several of the nurse's friends held an impromptu séance. They held hands, prayed and chanted for her to acknowledge them in the quiet stillness of the night shift. Suddenly, the lights in the room began flickering wildly, and thunder boomed from close by. Screaming wildly, the staff members ran in all directions and never attempted to contact the other world again. Their silent prayers for their departed friend would have to be enough (Johnston Memorial Hospital staff, 2004).

Sinking Spring Cemetery is filled with memories and history.

Ch. 4 Historical Tales and Frontier Stories

Stories, legends and historical accounts also become blended in and part of the oral history of a community. Although historical proof may not exist, many legends have been handed down in the community and became a part of the local folklore. These stories serve an important purpose, ranging from tightening community bonds to attempting to lay claim to some type of fame. The following stories are part of the history of Abingdon, and I've included them in this collection to help those who come after us remember the past.

Sinking Spring Cemetery

Named for the 1772 log church built by the Sinking Spring Presbyterian congregation, the cemetery has long been part of Abingdon's history. Large trees shade the quiet cemetery, which is an oasis of peace within Abingdon's busy downtown. Old limestone markers, some so eroded that the names have faded away, rise up among the more recent marble memorials. This old burial ground holds famous, and not so famous, people whose lives were devoted to improving the place they lived. According to the sketchy records, the grounds hold about 3000 marked graves and many unmarked ones. No records exist to identify the locations or occupants of the unmarked graves.

Every cemetery is dated by the year of its first interment. The first two people buried in the Sinking Spring cemetery, Henry Creswell and Frederick Mongle, were killed by Native Americans. Their stones are located near the tall column of the William King memorial. Although debatable, historians consider the grave of Henry Creswell to predate Mongle's burial by just a few months. Legend tells that a group of settlers left Black's Fort to visit their farms and were attacked by Indians. Henry Creswell was killed in this Indian attack at Piper's Hill. His crude tombstone reads, "Henry Creswell entered into this place July, 1776." A larger, more recent, memorial reads, "This monument was erected in 1913 by the citizens of Abingdon to mark the grave of Henry Creswell, who was killed by the Indians near this place and was the first person buried in this cemetery."

In 1776, Indians killed Frederick Mongle while he was guarding settlers picking chinquapins and flax at the current location of the Martha Washington Inn.

One of Abingdon's favorite boasts is of the number of "famous"

Unknown confederate dead section

people buried in this sacred ground. This plot of ground is the final resting place for several nationally known historical figures. Three former governors of Virginia, Gov. David C. Campbell (1837-1840), Gov. John B. Floyd (1849-1852), and Gov. Wyndham Robertson (1836-1837) are buried in the cemetery. Governor Floyd was also the Secretary of War under President Buchanan. Col. John Campbell, who was appointed U.S. Treasurer by President Andrew Jackson from 1829-1839, is buried in these grounds. The Parson Charles Cummings, famous as a fiery Presbyterian preacher, a Patriot, and Indian fighter, also was lain to rest here in 1812. William King, the Irishman who helped establish the Abingdon Male Academy and built the first brick house in town, is buried here. King was a wealthy landowner of the area, owing the saltworks in Saltville and several Abingdon businesses. King's marker is one of the more prominent, a tall white spire, standing above the others. The unknown Confederate dead were lain to rest in a fenced enclosure with a marker. Other local war heroes, men who fought in all the wars from the Revolutionary through Vietnam, have their final resting place in these grounds.

The most unusual tomb is a mound of stone covered with grass and with an interior iron gate. This resting place was constructed for John Henry and Melinda Martin, who died in the 1890s. Rumors explaining the unusual mound have flourished through the years. The most common story is that Mr. Martin wanted to be buried standing up so that he could keep an eye on his properties along Valley Street (Crabtree, 2003). This type of mausoleum was in style during that time period, so the story is debatable.

Other interesting markers include the following designs: a willow tree, a symbol of grief in the 19th century; a star, an early Christian symbol; a dove, a symbol of the Holy Spirit and peace; ivy leaves, symbolic of eternal life; flowers as symbols of the resurrection; harps, representing joy in Heaven and various Federal and Greek Revival artistic details such as medallions, swags, classical urns, and pilasters. The decorative elements of gravestones are also useful in identifying the dates they were erected (Summers 1989:230-233; Angle 1996; King

1994:117; "A Self-Guided Tour of Sinking Spring Cemetery.")

I enjoy reading tombstone inscriptions and have included several unusual ones from this cemetery:

Nancy J. Addison
Born July 30, 1821(?)
Died March 4, 1889
"Affliction sore for years I bore,
Physicians were in vain,
At length God pleased to give me ease
And freed me from my pain."

In memory of our sister,
Maria Anastasia King
Died at Martha Washington College,
Abingdon, Virginia
Dec. 19, 1861, aged 15 years
"Thy soul is in heaven,
They memory in the hearts
Of those who loved thee."

In memory of
Emma Johnston Brown
April 4, 1844
April 4, 1914
"Life's race well run,
Life's work well done,
Life's victory won,
Now cometh rest."

Parson Cummings Cabin

The Parson Cummings cabin, built in 1773, was later moved to the cemetery to be near the site of the Sinking Spring Presbyterian congregation's log church. Reverend Charles Cummings was known as the "Fightin' Parson," due to his participation in early battles on the frontier. The hardy minister would carry his shot pouch and rifle

Reverend Charles Cummings' cabin.

into church, walk to the pulpit, stand his rifle in the corner of the pulpit and preach his sermon. When someone teased him that carrying his rifle conflicted with the belief that no man should die before his time, Reverend Cummings replied, "Brother, if I meet an Indian and the Indian's time has come, I might thwart the will of the Lord if I failed to have my rifle with me with which to carry out His will." Parson Cummings has remained a historical icon and symbol of a brave pioneer in the area. Many of his descendents still live in the region and proudly lay claim to his blood line (Historical Society of Washington County, Virginia, 1968).

For years, the cemetery was neglected and in financial trouble. It was unclear who owned it and with no more plots to sell, no funds were available for upkeep and repair. For many years, a group of devoted ladies struggled to maintain it with the non-profit Sinking Spring Cemetery Association. The town did begin to maintain the community cemetery, and today, a lovely wrought iron fence encloses the sacred grounds.

As historic and full of memories as Sinking Spring cemetery is, it's surprising that there aren't more ghost stories. Some residents speak of seeing strange flickering lights and hearing footsteps behind them in the dark. Everyone agrees that only the brave of heart, or foolish, would risk spending the night there. I'm sure there is more local cemetery lore, especially as the grounds were a favorite hangout at night for children and teens with active imaginations. I admit to once walking the winding gravel road at night and hearing footsteps behind me. The footsteps would stop and continue each time I paused. As I squinted behind me through the humid summer dusk, I saw nothing but the leaves of the trees shaking in a sudden breath of wind. I heard a high-pitched tinkling noise, like a small bell, ring out from across the grounds. Needless to say, I ran out of the cemetery, never to enter it again after dark. It was only years later that I learned about an old Appalachian superstition that a ringing bell in a graveyard is the sign of a ghost. Even now, I'm not too proud to admit to having chills when I remember the incident.

Black's Fort: Haven in Frontier Days

It's hard to imagine this area as a dark wilderness, inhabited by wild beasts and Native Americans. But, this area was considered the western frontier for many years in the 1700s and 1800s, and Indian attacks were quite common. Treaties were made and broken on both sides, so blame shouldn't always be placed on the Native Americans. The natives were upset at losing their shared hunting grounds, and the idea of land ownership was foreign to them.

In fact, it's rare to talk to someone who doesn't have an ancestor who died in an Indian attack or an ances- *By DeAnna* tor captured and/or escaped from Indians somewhere *Akers Greene* back in her family tree. I admit that my family history has a story of a female ancestor from the Gilmer side who was captured by Indians. The story of Black's Fort is a favorite one in the area and was the subject of an outdoor drama, "The Fightin' Parson," which was staged near the fort's site as part of the Bicentennial celebration. My family played frontier folks in the play, and I was cast as a young pioneer girl captured by Indians in the drama, so Black's Fort holds a special fascination for me.

From 1754 to 1777, the frontier settlement population suffered from many Indian attacks. The Great Valley Road (today's US Rt. 11) was reported to be crowded with people leaving the area. The remaining brave pioneers near Abingdon decided they needed a shelter to protect themselves and their families. On July 20, 1776, a group of 500 settlers gathered at the farm of Capt. Joseph Black to build a fort for protection. Black's Fort was located on the west bank of Eighteen Mile Creek (Castle's Creek), near the present location of the trailhead of the Virginia Creeper Trail. The Reverend Charles Cummings offered a prayer before the residents begin to construct the stockade walls. The structure included only a few log cabins surrounded by a stockade. A sketch of the fort and the surrounding area even shows a possible water-filled moat surrounded by a palisade wall.

The first Washington County court was held at the fort on January 28th-January 29th, 1777. Settlers stayed in these frontier forts for protection from spring through fall from 1775 until the end of the Revolutionary War. The loss of the summer months for farming was costly for these farmers. Kindly citizens in Augusta County contributed money and provisions to assist these settlers, many of whom were their relatives. Black's Fort was prominent in the area from 1774 and for the next 100 years, as referenced in deeds and records. In 1879, Capt. Frank S. Findlay found remains of what many believed to be the fort while excavating on his property. Capt. Findlay uncovered a section of wall made from rock and logs. He discovered a white oak arrow stuck in a section of the wall.

A mystery has always surrounded the exact location of Black's Fort. Most researchers agreed the most likely location was at the site owned by the town just across the creek from the Virginia Creeper Train. In the late 1990s, Dr. Charles Bartlett conducted archeological excavations to find the location of the fort. This excavation showed major disturbances in the area; the topsoil had been removed, fill dirt and refuse buried, and then the top soil placed back over the fill. According to the excavation report, it's possible that part of the fort may be intact beneath the fill, but the site had been compromised severely (Summers 1989:257-260; Bartlett and Browning

1998; McConnell 1978).

Daniel Boone's Adventures in Wolf Hills

In 1760, Daniel Boone, his friend Nathaniel Gist, and a group of long hunters explored the Holston River Valley and camped in the area. One of their camps was said to be situated on a hill near the current location of the Cave House. As the men relaxed around campfires after a hard day of riding and hunting, wolves from a nearby cave began to circle the party. Slowly, the hungry wolves approached the camp and attacked the hunting party's dogs, killing and injuring many of them. After this attack, Boone decided the settlement's first name should be Wolf Hills. Boone remained in Abingdon to hunt and then continued along the Indian Trail toward Tennessee. A monument to this event stands in the front yard of the Cave House on Main Street in Abingdon. The "Wolf Cave" building behind the house covers the entrance to a large cave system. Reportedly, the underground network stretches from the Martha Washington, the Barter Theatre and several miles to the Acklin house, where General Morgan had his headquarters during the Civil War (Summers 1989:76).

Indians Kill Boone's Son near Castle's Woods

On September 25, 1773, several families traveled with Daniel Boone from their homes on the Yadkin River in North Carolina and passed through Abingdon and into the Powell Valley en route to Kentucky. While in the Powell Valley, a smaller scouting group led by James Boone, Daniel's eldest son,

Daniel Boone, frontiersman and hunter, traveled through Abingdon.

went ahead of the other travelers. A group of Shawnee and Cherokee Indians came upon the scouting party. James Boone and the others probably were not afraid since the Indians had pledged peace with the settlers. However, on October 10th, the Indians reneged on their peace treaty, and the entire group with James Boone was captured, tortured and killed. After this, Daniel Boone and family stayed to mourn at William Russell's house near Castle's Wood on the Clinch River. The Boone family stayed through the winter of 1773 and 1774. The Kentucky wilderness was still calling Boone, and eventually he made it to the promised land (Summers 1989:143).

By DeAnna Akers Greene

Overmountain Men and their Long Journey

One of the most amazing stories from our local history is the Revolutionary War tale of the "Over the Mountain Men." In 1780, British Col. Patrick Ferguson warned the backwoodsmen of this region to stop fighting the British, or "I will march my army over the mountains, hang your leaders, and lay your entire country to waste with fire and sword." Even back then, the mountain men in this area didn't take kindly to being threatened, and 400 volunteers from Washington County answered the call from Colonel William Campbell to defend the country's freedom. This group gathered near Wolf Creek at the Retirement house and traveled to Sycamore Shoals on the Watauga River (three miles from today's Elizabethton) to join frontiersmen from eastern Tennessee.

On September 26, 1780, the volunteer army of 1,040 men, bearing knives, tomahawks and long rifles, gathered at Sycamore Shoals and were blessed by local Reverend Samuel Doak. These brave "Overmountain" men marched over 200 miles to South Carolina to defeat the British at the Battle of King's Mountain, a turning point in our country's battle for independence. The battle lasted only 50 minutes, and Col. Ferguson was "handily" shot by a frontier fighter. Legend has it that the jubilant soldiers urinated on his grave site, which is located at the foot of the mountain. Sadly, many of the brave mountain men paid the price for freedom with their lives and were lain to rest in the North Carolina clay far from their homes.

One family legend is that Lieutenant Rees Bowen took his young son, John, with him on the over mountain journey and to the Battle of King's Mountain. After his father died in the battle, young John brought his father's bloody shoes home to his mother. Imagine the grief of the family, mixed with the joy to welcome home the young boy.

Another oral tradition from the battle is told about William Moore, a brave Washington County soldier who lost a leg and suffered a severe wound to his arm in the fighting. Moore was left to recover in safety in North Carolina. When Moore's wife heard of her husband's wounds, this brave woman traveled alone on horseback from Washington County to North Carolina in the cold month of November. Mrs. Moore cared for her husband until he regained his strength and then brought him back home. The tales of bravery and sacrifice of those in the American Revolution are numerous (Summers 1989:304-341).

Today, the Overmountain Victory Trail Association sponsors a reenactment of the march tracing the approximate route to King's Mountain. The association members stop at schools and museums along the way to conduct educational programs and set up interpretive camps. Blair Keller, a Washington County native, has participated in the march for many years and has fascinating stories to tell of his experience.

Conflicts with Native Americans

As land prices in the Shenandoah Valley, Pennsylvania and Maryland became more expensive, settlers began to look south for cheaper land and better opportunities. In 1745, James Patton secured a grant from the Governor of Virginia for 120,000 acres of land west of the Blue Ridge. In 1748, Patton and Dr. Thomas Walker of

By DeAnna Akers Greene

Albemarle County traveled with a group of surveyors and hunters to survey these lands in Patton's grant. In 1749, the Loyal Land Company sent Dr. Walker westward to survey lands to sell to settlers. Walker's journal of his travels provides a fascinating glimpse into conditions in this wilderness area. After 1753, the Loyal Company began to sell settlers tracts of land at the cheap price of three pounds per 100 acres.

As the frontier settlers moved into the lands along the Holston Rivers, they encountered resistance from Native American tribes, such as the Cherokee and Shawnee, who viewed the land as communal hunting grounds. Native Americans couldn't understand the European form of land ownership and conflicts over rights to use the land emerged. In fact, a Cherokee legend similar to the Garden of Eden story explained that the Holston Valley provided "too easy" a living for the Cherokee, so the spirits forced the people to leave. Because of cordial relationships with the Cherokees, at first the Native American attacks were mainly by Shawnees and Hurons. But by 1758, the Cherokees were also becoming more hostile. Between 1754 and 1763, during the French and Indian War, attacks were so numerous that land surveys were halted and many families left southwest Virginia.

In fact, the raids in 1755 were so atrocious, with many settlers killed and taken prisoner, that the frontier line was pushed back to the New River. Government reports were full of accounts of hundreds of settlers killed. The border became deserted. Treaties for peace were forged, but often ignored. In 1761, the states of Virginia and South Carolina launched attacks against the Cherokee homeland on the Little Tennessee River.

By 1776, fearful settlers had built a total of 23 forts along the waters of the Holston and Clinch rivers for protection from the

Indians. Until the end of the Revolutionary War, the settlers were forced to remain in the forts from early spring until late fall, which made agriculture and forest clearing difficult. During the Revolutionary War, the British often sent Cherokee and Shawnee groups to attack the outlying hinterland settlements. Finally, the Native Americans stopped their struggles to recapture southwest Virginia, and the pioneers were able to return.

About 1769, settlers began to move back into what later became Washington County. However, the more remote areas of southwest Virginia closer to Kentucky were still at risk. In 1784, many Indian attacks occurred in Powell's Valley and on the Wilderness or Kentucky Road. Isolated raids still occurred in the area, even as late as 1794 (Aronhime, February 10, 1980; Summers 1989:93-130; and Neal 1977:43-52)

By DeAnna Akers Greene

Indian Trails and Indian Olympics near Glade Spring

Indian trails, based on animal paths, were the first crude pathways into this wilderness. Indians traveled along the highlands and avoided crossing water. Early settlers followed one of these paths, when they left Seven Mile Ford, through the Byars Farm near Glade Spring, then near Meadowview and through present day Abingdon into Tennessee. Indians placed piles of stones along the paths, perhaps for superstitious reasons. One mound was located on the main road as it passes through Little Moccasin Gap.

Near Abingdon, another trail came in from the northwest. This trail crossed into the Kentucky at Cumberland Gap, a path followed by subsequent generations of migrating settlers, which was later called the Wilderness Road.

A small Indian mound and remains of an old Indian village were found at the present site of Kilmakronen, on the north and south side of the Middle Fork of the Holston River. Another Indian mound was located on the former Mahaffey farm about six miles southeast of Abingdon.

In the gentle hills south of the Old Glade Presbyterian Church near Glade Spring, a Native American gathering was known as "The Olympics of the Harvest Moon." Several early explorers note the event in their travel journals and it probably continued until the early 1700s.

The Olympic event occurred in the last part of October or early November. The Old Glade area was a natural location for the event, since several game and Native American trails intersected in the area. The Great Warrior Path ran roughly along Route 11, from Pennsylvania, through the Shenandoah Valley, into southwest Virginia and eastern Tennessee. Another trail connected from Ohio, through West Virginia, through gaps in the Clinch Mountains, Tazewell, Saltville, Old Glade and south into North Carolina. Since many Native tribes traveled and hunted through the area, the Old Glade area was a natural meeting place and the competition evolved. The location of precious salt in nearby Saltville also brought many natives to the area.

Early accounts note that 20 to 30 tribes participated in these games, and they traveled from North Carolina, South Carolina, West Virginia, Ohio and Kentucky. The games included competitions such as archery, running races, long and high jumping, horse riding and throwing rocks. Each tribe had trials to produce a representative to compete (Williams, 2003; Education Committee of Historical Society of Washington County, Virginia; Summers 1989:29).

Scalpings in Downtown Abingdon

Disregard the noisy bustle of downtown Abingdon, and try to imagine the land without buildings, roads, cars, or people. Picture the rolling fields and tall trees, and look around cautiously for wolves, panthers, and Native Americans hiding in the high grass. In 1776, the area where the Martha Washington Inn currently is located was a thick field of chinquapin and the land between there and Black's Fort (near the Virginia Creeper Trail entrance) was planted in flax. The chinquapin shrub is a type of chestnut with edible nuts. Flax was important to the early settlers, because they could pick it, spin it and weave it into fabric.

One warm summer day, a group of two men and three women were picking flax near Black's Fort. Frederick Mongle was stationed as the watch in case of Indian attack and all seemed quiet and peaceful. However, the Indians were hiding in the vegetation, and they surprised Mongle and scalped him. The other group members were able to run for the fort to safety. The pioneers from Black's Fort drove the Indians off. Mongle died from the severe wounds and was buried in Sinking Spring cemetery in Abingdon. Most historians believe his tombstone to be the second oldest in the graveyard. (Summers 1989:232-233, 257).

Major Indian Battle Fought on Middle Fork of Holston River

Although many have heard about the Indian battle at Long Island Flats in 1776, only a few people know of a battle fought after that near Kennedy's Mill. According to Aronhime, this battle was the only one fought on the Holston River north of the present-day Tennessee boundary. This battle also helped to end the Cherokee attacks in the area. Today, this pasture along the Middle Fork seems peaceful, but blood stains the soil here.

Letters from military commanders in 1776 report the Indians killing, destroying crops, and burning buildings up the Holston as far as present day Green Spring. All the forts were full of terrified settlers. These forts included Black's Fort (Abingdon), Bryant's Fort (U.S. 11 and Route 694), Snodgrass's Fort (Rt. 735 near Holston) and Kincannon's Fort (junction of U.S. 11 and Route 91). On a hot day in July, 1776, the pioneers hiding in Black's Fort were nervously waiting for scouts to return. Finally, the six men returned and reported the location of a camp of 40 braves (some accounts report only 25) near William Kennedy's mill. The people of Black's Fort sent messages to the other forts in the area asking for assistance in attacking the Indians. A force of 100 of the settlers traveled at night along today's Route 707 to take the Indians by surprise. When the settlers

Site of a clash between settlers and Native Americans.

arrived, the Cherokee were skinning a beef. A short battle took place, and the settlers killed every Native American, except for one. A long trail of blood led from the camp to the river, where many of the Indians drowned. Colonel William Snodgrass proudly reported that they took seven scalps as revenge (Aronhime, August 17, 1980).

Indian Attack at Douglas Wayside

In 1790, the settlers discovered plans for an Indian attack, and the outlying settlement areas needed to be warned. A young man named Douglass (the original spelling) who lived in Abingdon volunteered to travel to Castle's Woods (Castlewood) to warn the pioneers there. His friend, Benham, (today's Benham community is named for him) volunteered to accompany him on this treacherous journey through the mountains.

Douglass and Benham set out from Abingdon heading up the pass through the mountains. The two men stopped at a large table-like rock on the old road through Little Moccasin Gap, perhaps to take a break and eat. Suddenly, they heard a shot, and Douglass fell down. Smoke from the rifle could be seen rising from nearby trees. Knowing that his wound was fatal, Douglass told Benham to continue on to warn the settlers. Douglass aimed at the spot where he could

Picnic shelter marks the site of John Douglas' bravery.

see the smoke and started shooting, allowing Benham to slip away. Luckily, Benham was able to reach Castle's Woods safely and warn the settlers. Frontiersmen later found Douglass' body, which had been scalped. They buried him near the large rock. For years, people traveling by would drop a pebble upon the mound to honor his memory. Sadly, the road was constructed over the slight rise marking his resting spot. The Douglas Wayside rest stop along Highway 58/19 was named for this brave settler. The large rock where he was killed is still located at the site (Summers 1989:429).

Close Call at Smith Log Cabin

An old log house stood on Island Road just west of the intersection with Wagner Road near Bristol. This road was the main stagecoach route from Abingdon to Knoxville and the house served as a stagecoach stop for weary travelers. Gordon Aronhime wrote in a 1963 story in the *Bristol Herald Courier* about how the house was carefully dismantled to be reconstructed at another location. The house had a fine stone chimney and the interior stairs wound around the central chimney to an upper floor.

This log house was also significant because one of the last Indian attacks in Washington County occurred there on April 4, 1794. The story was told to Aronhime in 1963 by Mrs. Garnett Clayman, whose grandfather survived the incident. Ephraim Smith and his family had lived here in the valley since about 1773. Ephraim Smith was married to the daughter of Isaac Baker, who along with General Shelby had bought the Sapling Grove tracts where Bristol now stands. On the morning of April 4th, 1794, Smith, along with his sons, servants and slaves, were working hard in the fields. His wife, Ellen Baker Smith stayed in the cabin and watched their baby, Isaac, crawling on the floor.

The Smith family was fortunate to have a roan horse with a repu- tation for smelling nearby Indians. The horse had warned them before by kicking and bucking when Native Americans were nearby. This equine warning system proved reliable once again on this April morning when the roan began creating a violent stir.

Ellen peered out a small window and to her horror, saw a group of Indians approaching the cabin, with guns and tomahawks in hand. She had no gun in the house and knew the men were too far away to hear any cries for help. She looked at her baby crawling on the floor and had a desperate idea. The floor was a puncheon floor, which means that it was composed of halves of logs set loosely at the ends of the room. The flat side of the half log was the surface of the floor. When the Indians burst inside the house, nobody was visible. From her hiding place, Ellen could hear the heavy footsteps and the foreign talk of the natives. This enterprising young mother had lifted a plank from the puncheon floor and she and Isaac lay under the logs. When Isaac began to cry, she stuffed her apron in his mouth, and they both lay still and silent. Suddenly, she heard a voice say in English, "There's nobody at home." With dread, she realized this was the infa- mous Chief Benge. Benge was a half-breed who led war parties on attacks all over southwest Virginia. The Indians rummaged in the house and took some items with them and left. Ellen noticed the trusty horse had calmed down after they left the farm, but to be safe, she lay with her baby for another hour under the floor.

The Smith family later learned just how lucky they had been. Soon after their visit to the Smith farm, Chief Benge and his group had traveled to Scott County and attacked the home of Peter Livingston, killed family members and took others as prisoners. People said Ellen Smith gave thanks everyday to God for their escape from the Indians. It is unknown where the old house was reconstructed, but let's hope that it sits in a safe spot and keeps its memories of the brave Ellen Smith with it (Aronhime, March 10, 1963).

Livingston Family Attacked in Mendota

The following story chronicles the capture and escape of an early settler, as well as the capture and execution of the dreaded Chief Benge.

William Todd Livingston was one of the earliest settlers in Washington County. His son, Peter, inherited the rich farmland from his father, near the present community of Mendota. In 1794, Elizabeth Livingston was home alone when she saw seven Native Americans sneaking up to their house. Her husband, Peter and his brother Henry were working at a barn some distance away. She immediately took her three young children inside and locked the door. When they were unable to break through the door, the Indians set a nearby building on fire and the smoke forced Mrs. Livingston and her family outside. The Indians also captured her other children, her sister-in-law, and three slaves. The Native Americans particularly valued any African-American slaves they could capture. According to Mrs. Livingston's account of the attack, she was happy to see her house and its belongings burn, rather than be ransacked by the Indians. When the Indians were distracted by dividing the belongings they could steal, she had her eldest daughter take the baby and run toward their neighbor, John Russell's home.

The Native Americans took Mrs. Livingston and her family as captives and forced them at a brisk pace across Clinch Mountain. Mrs. Livingston learned that Benge, the savage Indian chief, was the leader of the party. He planned to take them to the Cherokee towns and trade them. As the group traveled into Wise County, near Stone Mountain, a group of Lee County militia led by Lieutenant Vincent Hobbs surprised the Indians. The soldiers killed Chief Benge with their first volley. The other Indians attempted to kill Mrs. Livingston with a tomahawk blow to the head. Five Indians escaped, taking one of the African-American slaves. The scalp of Chief Benge was sent to the Governor of Virginia. As a reward, Lieutenant Hobbs was awarded a handsome silver mounted rifle. A creek in Wise County still bears the name of Benge, for the Indian chief. This attack may have been the last recorded Native American attack on the settlers in southwest Virginia (Summers 1989: 439).

Fannie Dickinson Scott's Long Journey Home

This story of a frontier woman's incredible fortitude and bravery was often heard in the past, but is told less and less. This account may add it to the bedtime stories of local children again.

The peaceful valley between Powell's mountain and Wallen's Ridge in Lee County was the home of many early settlers. One of the early settler families in this valley was Archibald Scott and his wife Fannie Dickinson Scott. Fannie was descended from the brave pioneers of Castle's Woods. In 1782, Mr. Scott planted ten acres of corn and received 100 acres of land as part of the "corn right law." The family farmed along the banks of the Holston and forged a hard living from the soil. They built a blockhouse, which became known as "Scott's Station." By 1785, the Scott family included five children under the age of 8 years.

On June 20, 1785, the day seemed to be a typical one for the family. They worked in the fields all day and went to bed early. However, a band of about 20 Shawnee Indians had been watching the family and planning an attack. That night, the leader, Benge, the well-known half-breed, led this band to attack the pioneer family who were living in their hunting area.

The natives attacked and killed Mr. Scott first. The Indians also scalped and killed the five children, even as their mother begged for their lives. Fannie was taken prisoner and forced to travel with them on the long journey back to Ohio. It is said that when she didn't walk quickly enough, they slapped her in the face with the bloody scalps of her husband and children. Her endurance and courage along the exhausting journey surprised the Shawnees. The braves pushed Fannie onward for 200 miles until a stop to hunt in Kentucky, near the Ohio River.

Because they were impressed with Fannie's fortitude, the group decided that one of them would take her as his wife. This man was appointed her guard while the others hunted for game. Fannie was clever and determined to escape and go home. She made a rabbit stew for the brave, and sneaked in an herb she had secretly gathered. The herb was used to relieve pain in small does, but she knew it could be deadly in large does. After eating the stew, the Indian passed out and Fannie managed to escape. Fannie waded through streams to hide her trail and walked through deep forests for weeks. She ate roots, bark and berries for minimal sustenance. At one point, she heard an Indian hunting party nearby and she hid in a hollow log. Upon hearing a band of Indians and dogs, she found refuge in a hollow sycamore tree.

Finally, after days of wandering through the woods, Fannie came to a fork in the path, but didn't know which one was the way home. She decided to take the left fork, but after a short distance, she saw a bluebird. The bluebird flew by, touched her on the shoulder, and flew back and landed on the other path. Fannie thought nothing of the bird's strange actions and continued until the bluebird approached her again. Fannie believed it might be the spirit of her husband and children trying to help her back home. She backtracked and chose the other path which proved to be the right one. The path led her to Pound Gap where she rested and recovered from her long journey. She then returned to Castle's Woods where many of her relatives lived. After a few years, Fannie married Thomas Johnson and had other children. She lived to an old age and her ashes rest on a hill not far from the base of Clinch Mountain in Hayter's Gap (Historical Society of Washington County, Virginia Education Committee; Summers 1989:376-379).

Confederate Veterans Reunion, June 3, 1914. (Courtesy Historical Society of Washington County, Virginia)

Ch. 5 "The War of Northern Aggression"

Visitors or "transplants" moving to many areas of the south often comment that the Civil War seems to live on here, while it's been forgotten by northerners and folks from other areas. Perhaps, it's because the losers rarely forget a battle or that the lean Civil War years and reconstruction were so hard on the population. Regardless of the reason for retaining this fascination, the "War of Northern Aggression" is a common theme in folk tales, ghost stories and oral histories of the area.

The Civil War was a time of chaos in this particular region, mainly because the saltworks in nearby Saltville were a target for Federal troops. These saltworks provided necessary salt for the Confederate army and most of the region. The Virginia and Tennessee Railroad was also a target for the Northern Army. By 1863, the population was starving and appealed to Richmond for help. In 1863, the county was full of stragglers and deserters from the Confederate army.

Unfortunately, these men claimed to belong to a cavalry and traveled through the county robbing people of food, money, horses, and clothing. The unrest and dangerous atmosphere prompted the local government to organize a company for home defense in June, 1863.

By January 1864, Washington County had supplied at least 2000 soldiers to the army of the Confederate States. Several groups of Confederate troops were quartered nearby and used much of the food and forage in the area. In December, 1864, federal troops under General Stoneman were approaching Abingdon on their way to Saltville from East Tennessee. Having heard stories of marauding soldiers, the local people panicked. Roads were blocked with citizens, livestock, wagons and buggies fleeing the approach of the troops. Abingdon was deserted, with only a few elderly folks, women and children remaining.

Several stories live on as local lore about General Stoneman's raid through southwestern Virginia. For the most part, according to historical accounts, the Yankees took only supplies they needed and didn't burn private houses. Several families do have their own stories of Yankee cruelties and encounters with renegade Confederate soldiers which have been handed down through the years (Summers 1989:530-532).

Confederate Deserter Shot

Across the street from Sinking Spring Cemetery is the historic African-American cemetery. It was neglected for many years, and I remember as a child noticing how the tall grass and weeds almost covered the tombstones. Fortunately, today, the African-American plot is maintained just as well as its neighboring graveyard across Russell Road.

An interesting occurrence happened there during the Civil War. According to L.C. Angle, a man from Wise County deserted the Confederate Army and then crossed over and joined the Union troops. Confederates captured he soldier, and he was sentenced to be shot. The deserter was shot on a hill near town, which ironically later became the African-American cemetery. However, he wasn't buried in nearby Sinking Spring cemetery, because in those days, if you had committed a crime, you could not be buried in a public cemetery. No documentation of his final resting place remains (Angle, 2004).

1908 Dedication of Confederate Soldier Memorial (Courtesy Historical Society of Washington County, Virginia.)

Elderly Resident Shows Yankees Southern Grit

Fortunately, this Civil War story has a happy ending and reflects the fortitude and courage of females left to face the Yankees alone during those years. The story comes from the published reminiscences of Robert M. Hughes and describes his family's encounter with the Yankees during Stoneman's Raid. Picture a fearful household in Abingdon on December 14, 1864 when the Yankees arrived in town. The gentlemen of the household, several of them wounded, had escaped to the mountains just before the Union troops came into town. Left in the small farmhouse were the niece of Joseph E. Johnston (mother of Robert M. Hughes), Sally Hampton (daughter of Wade Hampton), a young Robert M. Hughes, and Mrs. Floyd, grandmother of Robert Hughes and the widow of John B. Floyd. It was said that the Yankees hated the late John B. Floyd more than any other man in the Confederacy, so the household was particularly worried about their treatment by the troops. If the Yankees knew their identities, the women knew the house would be burned down, and they would likely be mistreated.

The raiders came during the middle of the night and camped near the house. The family sat up all night fully dressed and waiting in the sitting room. Robert Hughes wrote of donning three suits of clothes to save them from a possible house fire. Mrs. Floyd was especially very nervous. Finally, early in the morning a group of Union soldiers approached the front door. Robert Hughes recalled the conversation as follows:

"Good morning, gentlemen, won't you get down?" asked Mrs. Hughes (Robert's mother).

"What do you mean by calling them gentlemen?" asked Mrs. Floyd.

"Aunt Sally, why shouldn't I call them gentlemen? They have done nothing to make me think they are not gentlemen," replied Mrs. Hughes.

"Are there any rebels or traitors in the house?" barked out a Yankee officer.

"If you mean by that the gentlemen of the house, they heard you were coming and have escaped to the mountains. But I have no objection to your searching the house. Won't you get down and do so?" said Hughes' mother.

"If you give me your word, Madam, that there are no men in the house, I will not search it," replied the kind officer.

"I give you my word, but I do not mind your searching it if you will have reliable men to do it. I have had all the flour and meal baked into bread for you, and there are some hams and bacon in the smokehouse. Won't you give me a guard and make them leave some of the meat for me and my children?" said Mrs. Hughes.

Naturally, the Yankees took the offered food and horses.

Hughes remembers the Yankees leaving without searching the house, and the household was relieved the troops didn't burn the house. As the soldiers passed by, elderly Mrs. Floyd stood up with dignity, shook her small fist at them, and uttered curse words that had never been heard from her mouth. One of the soldiers laughed and said, "Old woman, keep your temper." (Hughes 1936:1-13)

Confederate Soldier monument in original position in center of Main Street. (Courtesy Historical Society of Washington County, Virginia)

Burning of Abingdon

That same day, December 14, 1864, would live on in the memories of Abingdon's residents, because Federal guns were heard on the western end of Abingdon. One can only imagine the fear, confusion, and dread that all the residents felt as the "Northern Aggressors" approached.

The Confederates, part of General Duke's command, were camped at the James A. Bailey farm a few miles northeast of Abingdon. The Confederate soldiers tried to delay the Yankees, but were vastly outnumbered. The federal troops approached on Main

Street, and their guns dispersed the Confederate men. Gen. Stoneman took possession of the town and burned the Virginia Tennessee Depot, Hurt's store, Sinon's wagon shop, Mussers' wagon shop, and the county jail and barracks opposite the jail, at the corner of Court and Valley streets. Per Stoneman's instructions, the soldiers burned all buildings that were either occupied by Confederate officials or used to store confederate supplies.

The Union officers had told the troops not to enter private houses or plunder any other buildings in town. To their credit, witnesses reported that the soldiers placed wet blankets on the roofs of the adjacent houses to prevent fires from spreading from targeted buildings. However, according to one story, the Union army's patience must have worn thin amidst the chaos. The Yankees also planned to burn an old tobacco warehouse, located across from the courthouse. An elderly African-American man was hiding in the warehouse, but the Yankees wouldn't let him come out. The old man was burned to death in the warehouse.

Another story shows the stubborn pride prevalent in residents of small southern towns, and especially Abingdon. While the Yankee troops were in Abingdon, they stretched a US flag from the Courthouse across Main Street. The people of Abingdon were so stubborn that they used the parallel side streets to avoid walking under the flag. To make it worse, these streets weren't macadamized and were full of mudholes.

The following story is the most often repeated Civil War story and is still told in a tone of outrage. Unfortunately, after the main troops left to continue on to Saltville, several stragglers stayed behind to have their horses shod. A man named James Wyatt, a former resident of Abingdon who had joined the Union Army, led the miscreants. Wyatt was from this area and felt he had been treated unfairly under apprenticeship to Gabriel Stickley. After the main troops left, Wyatt rode his horse down Main Street, and stopped at the lovely Washington County Courthouse. He then set it on fire, as well as all the buildings on the south side of Main Street. The fire destroyed all the buildings on both sides of Main Street from Court Street to

Brewer Street. Wyatt then stopped his horse at the intersection of Main and Court streets in front of the Nidermaier & Barbee store and gleefully watched the fire. Wyatt would not allow anyone to put out the fire.

While the renegade Yankees were burning houses, a party of Confederates disguised in federal uniforms approached on horseback along Main Street. They pursued Wyatt and his compatriots to the campus of Martha Washington College. Finally, a Confederate pistol found its mark, and Wyatt was shot from his horse. Wyatt was carried to the College gymnasium and died there about midnight. This story is the explanation for the ghost horse seen by many galloping across the Martha Washington Inn grounds on moonlit nights. Today, Abingdon residents still bear a grudge against the Yankees for losing their courthouse and many of the historic buildings near the area (Summers 1989:541-543; Angle 1996; Hughes 1936).

Named the Yankee Baby

Although handed down through oral history, this tale of the Yankee Baby was lost in the dusty pages of history for many years. It's a charming story and well worth resurrecting.

John Kreger, the clerk of court in Abingdon, kept his office on the same lot as his house. Built in 1836 by Andrew Gibson, the house was located on the corner of Main and Pecan streets. The house was historically known as Villadoe, and today is called Rainero. During the Dec. 14th 1864 Yankee raid of Abingdon, they planned to burn John Kreger's office, next to his house, to destroy records. Mr. Kreger's wife had just had a baby and was "abed" with the newborn. Kreger tearfully begged the Yankees not to burn the office because it might set his house ablaze and would surely kill his family. The Yankees agreed not to burn the house, probably saving the mother's and child's lives.

Unfortunately, as fate would have it, the child received the nickname the "Yankee Baby," a heavy burden to bear during Reconstruction. According to the story, this "unlucky" baby grew up to a fine gentleman, John M. Kreger, the father of Mrs. Virginia

Historical photo of Villadoe or Rainero (Courtesy Historical Society of Washington County, Virginia)

Rainero as it appears today

Witherspoon. (Angle 1996:109; Historical Society of Washington County, Virginia 1968:7-8).

Lure of the Bank's Gold

Whenever there's a Civil War story, there's bound to be some treasure involved. Here's one story that, once again, has a happy ending for all involved.

The Bank is one of the more fascinating, and well-preserved buildings in Abingdon and is located just east of the Washington County Courthouse. Built in 1858, the imposing brick building was constructed to be both a bank and residence and is now a National Historic Landmark. The front street windows on the bank side of the building still have the iron bars from the original bank design. Barred double doors also divide the bank from the remainder of the house, where the banker usually lived. The property owners have retained and preserved the stone vault and counting room in the house.

According to legend, the Union soldiers dug up the brick floor of the vault to try to find the bank's gold during Stoneman's Raid on Abingdon. Fearing the Union's advance, Robert R. Preston, the banker, had buried the gold in the side yard. Through southern ingenuity, the gold remained hidden and helped fund the reconstruction in the area.

Another Civil War story from Stoneman's Raid is told about a drunken Yankee soldier who entered the Bank building looking for money. When the family told the soldier that they had no money, the soldier broke into the ill Mr. Preston's bedroom and threatened to kill him. Fortunately, Mr. Preston's daughter found a Union officer on the street to intervene. A gentleman despite his political views, the Union officer forcefully escorted the drunken soldier out of the house and arranged a suitable punishment. The gallant officer also placed a guard around the house which saved it from being burned. I wish I could say the soldier and Mr. Preston's daughter then fell in love and lived happily ever after, but that would be inventing history (Historical Society of Washington County, Virginia 1968:16-18).

General Morgan's (First) Funeral in Abingdon

Many residents of the area may not know that Abingdon was the site of the famous Confederate General John H. Morgan's funeral ceremony and (first) burial. 'Tis a sad story, but one full of twists and turns. The bridge across the railroad tracks near Acklin was named

Acklin, used by General John H. Morgan during the Civil War.

the John Hunt Morgan Memorial bridge in his honor.

Residents of this area respected General Morgan because of the service he provided to the Confederacy. During the summer of 1864, General Morgan used the Acklin house, located on the east end of Main Street, as his headquarters when 5000 of his calvary were camped in Abingdon. According to legend, the General and his troops used the underground cave system beneath Abingdon to travel to different locations during the war.

Known as the "Thunderbolt of the Confederacy," General Morgan always dressed in uniform, with tall boots and a felt hat with one side turned up. The Confederacy loved him for his pranks, courage and daring. But, to the Union, he was "Morgan the Raider" and "King of the Horse Thieves." In September 1864, General John Hunt Morgan was betrayed and murdered in Greenville, Tennessee. The federal troops threw his body over a horse and paraded it through the town. General Morgan's body was embalmed and brought back to Abingdon where Mrs. Morgan was staying with relatives. His funeral procession in Abingdon was held at the Lutheran Church and extended almost two miles, with a hearse, chaplains, family, military members, military court, officers, privates, and thousands of citizens. Strangely, in a similar fashion to the story of the crucifixion of Christ, legend says that sundown on that day was one of the blackest and strangest ever seen.

The General's body was interred in Sinking Spring cemetery,

although not for long. The city of Richmond notified the town that they wanted the general buried there, so his body was dug up after two days. His body was taken by train to Richmond, stopping at various stations for residents to pay respects. Finally, the deteriorating state of the embalmed body prevented any other train stops, and the train reached Richmond. General Morgan lay in state in Richmond for several days. He was then buried in Hollywood Cemetery where many of the confederate leaders were buried. It seems he couldn't rest there either because shortly afterwards the people of Kentucky took General Morgan's remains to be buried in Lexington.

There are stories that General Morgan and some of his soldiers have been seen at the Tavern and the Martha Washington Inn, perhaps traveling through the secret labyrinth of caves under the town (Angle 1996:108; King 1997:88; Summers 1989:533-534).

Retirement

Retirement, the imposing brick house located just off Colonial Road, has one of the more illustrious histories of any buildings in town. From the muster site of the Overmountain Men to an unsuccessful silk worm venture, the house could certainly tell some tales. Surely, some ghosts must frequent the house, but I could find no ghost stories about it. However, the wedding story that follows is one of the most commonly told stories of Civil War times in the area.

Retirement, built before 1815, site of much history.

According to land records, Captain Robert Craig completed the main section of the house before 1815. Captain Craig was one of the first trustees of the town and assisted with the planning of Abingdon. He attempted to begin silk manufacturing on the farm by growing silk worms, but the venture was not successful. A separate log kitchen was located close behind the main house. Additions have been constructed over the years, all in keeping with the original architectural style.

As one of the earliest houses in Abingdon, history left its mark here, too. Historians believe the meadow to the west of Retirement was the site of the muster grounds for the volunteer militia during the Revolutionary War. It was here in 1780, that Col. William Campbell summoned 200 of the local militia to march to Sycamore Shoals, near present-day Elizabethton, and then on to King's Mountain, South Carolina to help win the Battle of King's Mountain. This group of brave men was later called the Overmountain Men. The members of the Overmountain Victory Trail marchers gather at the meadow each fall to reenact the long march. It's also interesting that Union troops camped in the same meadow in 1864, and that soldiers of World War I and World War II also used it for overnight camps.

Wedding at Retirement Delayed Due to Yankees

Aunt Lou, a household slave from Retirement, told another early story about Retirement which happened during the Civil War. The wedding for Catherine Fulkerson, the resident of the house, and Floyd B. Hurt had been planned for December, 1864. Obtaining food and drinks to provide a wedding feast was no easy matter in those lean times of the Civil War. The family had gathered enough food for a meager wedding supper and invited many guests. However, news came that the Yankees were approaching Abingdon, and Floyd Hurt, who served with the Confederate States Depositary, left the house immediately. The weather was cold and snowy, and the Union soldiers were tired of their paltry food rations. When the hungry soldiers saw the wedding feast, the Yankees devoured all the food, even the wedding cake. Catherine barely managed to hide the family silver, and Aunt Lou hid a large ham. One could say that the house and its residents were lucky, since many buildings and the Courthouse in Abingdon were burned. The wedding had to be delayed, although it was held the following week.

Some versions of this story also include a curious ending. One of Catherine's brothers, Abram Fulkerson, served in the Virginia House of Delegates, the Virginia Senate and Congress. When talking to a fellow congressman in Washington, he mentioned where he had been born. The congressman from Illinois supposedly showed him a gold ring found in a slice of cake that he had eaten in Abingdon. Fulkerson told the man that the ring had been hidden in his sister's wedding cake, which was eaten by the Union soldiers. It was a tradition to hide a wedding ring inside a wedding cake and the person finding it would be the next one to be married. The congressman offered to return it, but Fulkerson explained that his sister had died and that he could keep it as a souvenir of Abingdon.

Another happier version of the end of this story is told by L.C. Angle in his oral history. About 20 years after the rescheduled wedding celebration, an Abingdon man went to Philadelphia to buy goods for his store. After introducing himself to the store owner, he modestly said, "I'm from a small town in southwest Virginia called Abingdon, although you've probably never heard of it." The Philadelphia storekeeper replied, "Yes, I have heard of it. I was with Stoneman when he came through the town. I have a ring that I found in a bite of wedding cake and I'd like to return it to Abingdon." So the wedding ring hidden inside the cake was returned to the Floyd family in Abingdon (Historical Society of Washington County, Virginia 2004; Angle 1996:105-106).

The Virginia Creeper Train near Abingdon (Courtesy Historical Society of Washington County, Virginia)

Ch. 6 Hauntings of Damascus, Rich Valley, Meadowview and Shortsville

Many consider Washington County to be one of the most scenic areas of Virginia. Drive its curvy roads, and you can see classic historic red brick houses, green hills dotted with cattle, and many unique communities with their own histories and stories. The peaceful atmosphere belies the ghost stories, mysteries and frightening legends which lie beneath. I've attempted to "mine" out some of these stories to illustrate the special history of this small region of southwest Virginia. I've arranged the stories by geographical location because of the importance of retaining the context and "fit to the land." I've included a liberal dose of history about the communities and buildings so that, you, the reader can take the historical background into consideration.

Creepy Virginia Creeper Trail

Most bikers and pedestrians who travel the Virginia Creeper Trail know little of its history and stories. The night-time bike rides along the trail might assume a different light once you read these tales. Stories are quite common about railroad lines all over the country, and Washington County is no exception. Rails seem to magnetically attract stories of ghosts and strange happenings.

In 1898, Wilton E. Mingea acquired the Virginia-Carolina Railway Company. Norfolk & Western Railway later purchased the railway and ran trains on it for many years. The rail began in Abingdon and followed sections of an old Indian trail to the small town of Todd, North Carolina. The hard work of hundreds of immigrant and black laborers resulted in the completion of miles of rail along the middle and south forks of the Holston, and through the River Knobs, the Watauga Valley and Great Knobs.

The first train "christened" the rail on February 7, 1900 and chugged the 16 miles from Abingdon to Damascus. Because the train struggled up the long hills and slowly rounded the curves, it earned the nickname, "Virginia Creeper," for the "V-C" initials on the train. Another explanation for the nickname is the widespread presence of Virginia Creeper vines along the tracks. Regardless of the name's origin, the Virginia Creeper name stuck and is still used today.

In 1977, the last train completed the trip, and the tracks were removed. For many years the rail line was deserted, and became overgrown with vegetation. In 1982, the town of Abingdon acquired a 34.3 mile section from the railroad company and turned it into a nature trail for walking and riding bikes and horses. As one of the first successful adaptive reuse projects for abandoned rail lines, the Virginia Creeper has been featured in *Southern Living* and other tourist publications. The "rails to trails" movement soon became popular all over the nation. Today, thousands of visitors enjoy the scenic beauty and historic experience of traveling the Virginia Creeper Trail. An exhibit of photographs of the rail line's history, taken by Winston Link, is located in the restored Abingdon Passenger station on Wall Street in downtown Abingdon. The building also houses the busy Historical Society of Washington County, trusted curators of a plethora of historical research material.

Railroad lines often beget old stories and legends, especially when the lines have been in place for many years. For the Virginia Creeper line, the story goes that many of the railroad workers were convicts working on chain gangs from local prisons, as well as immigrants. Many of these prisoners were African-Americans. The work was exhausting and dangerous, since they used black powder to blast through rock and dug rocks and earth with picks and shovels. Mules and horses hauled the heavy ties to the line, and the laborers set the ties. Due to the dangerous conditions, many convicts were injured, and several died because of the strenuous work pace. Perhaps some of them were beaten or shot to death by tough overseers anxious to speed up the pace. Legend has it that these prisoners' bodies would be unceremoniously dumped in shallow graves beside the tracks. These "on-site" graves were not marked or recognized in any way, and the remains lie forgotten even today.

Sometimes, late on a foggy night, stories say that these convicts walk along the Creeper Trail between Abingdon and Damascus, moaning their dismal fates in low rumbling tones. Some folks have mistaken the moans for a ghost train, but if you listen closely, you will hear these human sounds of mourning. Other brave souls out on the Creeper Trail at night have heard the ringing of sledgehammers on steel spikes and the chain gang's songs, as the ghosts of the suffering convicts keep working into eternity.

Another interesting story is that dogs will not enter the Creeper Trail at night. Perhaps due to their sensitive hearing, dogs seem to sense the restless souls whose bodies sleep in unmarked graves in the deep fill along the old Virginia-Carolina rail bed (McKinney, 2004; McGuinn 1998:1-9)

Thrifty Bill Musick of Rich Valley

G. Lee "Bud" Hearl is a storyteller in the Abingdon area who provides entertainment at many local events with his Appalachian stories and ghostly tales. His mother told him this story about a thrifty ghost in Rich Valley many years ago.

Bill and Malinda Musick lived near Rattle Creek in the hills above the Holston in Rich Valley. The couple vowed to work and climb out of poverty, even though they had no education or way to bring in extra money on their steep, hillside farm. But they worked from sunup to sundown and produced extra livestock and produce to sell or trade for supplies. The thrifty couple managed to save a moderate amount of money which in those days was in gold and silver coins. They faithfully placed the precious coins in a trunk hidden beneath the stairs in their house.

One cold winter night, a soot fire started in their chimney, and the first thing Bill did was drag their money trunk out of the house. Bill managed to pull the trunk several hundred feet down the hill and put it down at the old cemetery. It was only after doing this that he ran back to the house and yelled, "Malinda, get out of the house! It's on fire and burnin' up." Malinda calmly dipped the gourd dipper into the water bucket and threw the water into the fireplace. Luckily, the steam rose up the chimney and put the soot fire out. Relieved the fire had been put out, Bill now was worried about getting the trunk back up the hill into the house. Malinda went with him to carry it, but they couldn't carry its heavy weight up the hill. Afraid to leave their life's savings in the cemetery, Bill decided to stay outside and guard it until morning.

Poor Bill wrapped up in all of his clothes and a wool blanket, but didn't get much sleep in the cold. He heard the wind whistle around the tombstones and thought he heard voices coming from the graves. Morning finally came, and he fetched Malinda to guard the trunk. Bill went to find a neighbor to help carry it back to their house. As Bill and Malinda had children and grandchildren, they constantly reminded them of how you need to save every penny and deprive yourself to save. After long lives, the couple died and willed their small "fortune" to their children.

Their son and his wife moved into the old log house and liked to relax in front of the fireplace after their day was done. Each night when the clock struck nine, they would see the ghost of old Bill Musick appear at the foot of the stairs. Bill would glower at them and say, "You're burning too much oil. Time to blow out the lamp and git to bed." The couple said that if they didn't blow out the lamp, a breeze would spring up and blow the light out. They would then hear footsteps going back up the stairs. Sometimes, far into the night, the couple could hear a voice in the attic muttering, "Too much oil, too much oil." (Hearl, 2004)

Meadowview

The quiet community of Meadowview was called Meadow View (two separate words) until the 1930s. Native American trails passed near the later site of the town. The first settler was James Glenn, who purchased land in 1783. The community name may come from an early name of Meadow Mountain, shown for nearby Whitetop Mountain on the 1749 Peter Jefferson Map. Another explanation is that William Edmondson named his house Edmondson's Meadow and enjoyed looking at the numerous green meadows surrounding his house. Until the railroad's arrival in 1856, the town was small and remote. After the train arrived, stockyards and a transportation center were established in Meadowview to ship livestock, produce and goods to all over the eastern U.S. The town remained busy and active until the 1950s, when the departure of the train hurt the economy. The town is now a peaceful, mainly residential community, with a rich history (Williams and Wagner 1998).

Edmondson Hall

This stately home just outside Meadowview is one of those houses that you slow down to admire. The Salyers family has devoted much time and labor to restoring the house to its grandeur. If only they had known what company they would keep when they finally moved in, the Salyers might have changed their minds. People who have studied supernatural phenomena claim to feel the presence of spirits when they enter the house. However, the family maintains they have never felt threatened by any of the spirits who also call the house their home.

Built in 1856 just outside of Meadowview, this brick, Greek Revival house has withstood time very well. Fortunately, the owners

Edmondson Hall, built in 1856, one of the most haunted houses in the county.

have kept most of its original exterior and interior features. William Campbell Edmondson, an early pioneer and merchant in Meadowview, built the house, and the original parcel included 383 acres in this fertile valley. William Edmondson was also the first postmaster for Meadowview. Edmondson and Thomas W. Colley built the first general store in the town. Two slave cabins were formerly located on the property.

Historic houses often hold many memories, and Edmondson Hall is no exception. There are local stories about finding infant bones in the attic, of seeing a ghostly woman rocking in a rocking chair in a bedroom, and being chased from the yard by a mysterious rider on horseback. Several friends and members of the Salyers family have had odd experiences in the house, including hearing footsteps upstairs when nobody else is home, feeling cold areas in a certain upstairs bedroom, experiencing the feeling of being watched, and hearing unknown voices calling their name. Others have seen a ghostly figure dressed in white, which disappears. An interior decorator helping with the house even felt someone pull her hair in a front upstairs bedroom, when nobody was nearby. Another visitor felt someone grab her in an empty room.

Cynthia Salyer, the current owner, often hears someone pick up another phone extension when she is the only one home talking on the telephone. Her friends have heard these strange clicks also. Ms. Salyer also has noticed the smell of cooking food before, when no food was being prepared. She has seen a dark shadow following her daughter into the house. Ms. Salyer's experiences have been benign encounters, and she has never felt threatened by the odd happenings.

Another chilling story happened during the extensive house renovations the Salyers conducted. At that point, the family was sleeping downstairs in the dining room, since it was the only heated portion of the house. One night, Ms. Salyer woke up and saw a young child looking around the corner of the dining room at her sleeping family. The child appeared to be about 10 or 12 years old and wore a long white gown and had a Buster Brown type haircut. She looked at the boy, who remained silent and watched the family. Ms. Salyer thought it might be her elderly mother who sometimes wandered around the house at night. After falling back to sleep and then waking up again, she decided to go into the kitchen. She observed the child peering around the doorway for as long as it took her to smoke a cigarette. Baffled, she went back to sleep, since she didn't feel in danger. The next morning, when Ms. Salyers asked her mother if she had been up walking, her mother said she hadn't. Could it have been the spirit of a child who once lived in the house coming to meet the new owners?

Ms. Salyers, family members, and others visiting the house also have heard strange voices. But in this case, the voices seemed to try to warn her. One night about 10 p.m., Ms. Salyers, her daughter, and a nurse heard a man's loud voice calling Ms. Salyers' name. The women knew that neither Mr. Salyers nor her sons were home at the time. Suddenly, two light bulbs in the kitchen blew out. Energy fields can sometimes cause light bulbs to burst. Ms. Salyers heard a commotion from upstairs and fearing for her elderly, bedridden mother, the women ran upstairs. When they entered her mother's bedroom, the elderly lady had almost fallen out of her hospital bed. To this day, Ms. Salyers believes that the loud voice and the light bulbs were a warning to her of an impending danger to her mother.

Ms. Salyer has her elderly mother, known as Gma, living with her in the house. One day, the lady who helped Ms. Salyer clean the house commented that Gma didn't look as if she felt well. The older lady commented that she was glad all the folks walking around the dining room table all night were finally gone. She claimed to have seen identical twin girls, about 21 years old, that stayed in her room all night. The beautiful girls had long blonde hair, and one stood at the foot of her bed while the other stood at her bedroom door. The strangest thing is that the family found out later that twins had lived in the house. Gma said she wished they hadn't whispered so much all night because it had kept her awake.

Ms. Salyer and the cleaning lady were confused by Gma's stories but patiently listened to her. Later in the afternoon, Gma was downstairs for lunch when she looked at the front door. She said, "Who's that? We must have company. Oh no, they must have changed their mind because they're leaving now." The cleaning lady burst into tears, saying she had to go home. When she went home, she told her husband that she was worried that Gma was having a premonition because death always knocks at the door. Strangely enough, that night, Ms. Salyers heard a noise and found that Gma had fallen. The family called 911, and the doctors transferred Gma to ICU where they found a blood clot. Gma did almost die that night, but somehow she pulled through and recovered. Reflecting back on this, Ms. Salyers wonders if Gma really was having premonitions of her own death when she saw the various visitors. Fortunately, Gma recuperated and cheated the visitors who may have been bringing death.

Ms. Salyers only frightening encounter happened the first night when she was alone in Edmondson Hall. She was nervous because some neighborhood boys had been prowling on the property. She decided to sleep upstairs in a bedroom with double locks on the door to alleviate her nervousness. As she was dozing off, Ms. Salyers thought she saw a "furry" type of bird fly out of the closet and start to dive down on her. She blinked her eyes rapidly to check her vision. She then noticed a beautiful, tall woman dressed in clothing from the 1920s, standing at the foot of her bed. Ms. Salyers rubbed her eyes and sat up in bed, her heart racing. She didn't see any other apparitions, so she fell back to sleep. She didn't feel threatened by these appearances and hasn't been afraid to spend the night alone in the house (King 1994:122; Salyers, 2004).

Blacksburg Community

An African-American community has long been located in an area between Meadowview and Glade Spring on land originally part of the Colonel William Byars plantation. Former slaves from nearby Brook Hall established the community. The Brook Hall heirs gave the African-Americans land from their holdings and $20-$25 to begin independent lives, as well as $21 for funeral costs. The community is located along Indian Run and is considered the oldest and largest African-American settlement in the area. The valley contains rolling hills and rich farmland. Drovers once moved groups of turkeys, sheep, and cattle along an old trail through the area. One of the community's earliest settlers was a blacksmith, named Mr. Black, from which the community derives its name. The Mt. Zion Baptist Church in the community is the mother church of all the African-American Baptist churches in the area.

Today, between 15 and 20 African American families make their home in Blacksburg, although many descendents of the original families have left the community for economic opportunities elsewhere. Names of families who lived and still may live in Blacksburg include the following: Coleman, Gibbs, Boyd, Hill, Cato, Foster, Lampkin, Newton, Henry, and Poindexter.

In the past, many of the inhabitants of Blacksburg helped each other survive hard times, as they do today. One old man often hunted in the area and brought back game to share with the hungry in the community. He usually took his trusty beagle along for help with tracking and for protection against larger animals such as bear and wildcats. After one of his usual hunting trips, the kind old man didn't return. The community searched for him everywhere and finally found him. Someone had murdered the man and his beagle was stretched out dead beside him. The master and his trusty dog were both buried at the Blacksburg cemetery on the top of a nearby hill. Sometimes, violence can create restless spirits who can find no rest. It's said that, on the anniversary of the hunter's death, if you are in the lonely cemetery, you can hear his beagle barking, as if trying to warn him of the impending death. The dog's barking turns into howling as the dog mourns both of their unsolved deaths (Williams, 2004; VDHL 95-218).

Lady of the McConnell/Logan House

When I was gathering stories for this book, the McConnell/Logan house could easily have garnered the title of "Most Well-Known Haunted House. " Strangely, the story of the ghost lady at the window is also one of the few stories has been proven to be a hoax. But, Glenn Sexton provided me with his own "true" ghost story about the house, and he believes it to be true to this day.

The McConnell family had this two-story brick house built in 1892 on picturesque Lindell Road. Reportedly, the designer of this house was the same architect who designed the lovely Emory and Henry college campus. Other owners of the house through the years include the Campbell, Jameson, Logan and Litton families. Built to withstand many years, the walls of the house are four bricks deep on

McConnell/Logan House, built 1892

the first story and three bricks deep on the second story. Due to absentee owners, the house stood vacant for many years, so naturally several haunting stories surround this historic house.

The most commonly heard ghost story in Washington County is of a ghostly female figure that you could see peering from an upstairs window. Local folks would drive by just to look for the lady. Finally, the mystery was solved and written about by the late great Jack Kestner in his newspaper articles in the *Bristol Herald Courier*. The absentee owners had placed an advertising poster of a woman inside near an upstairs window. The lady could barely be seen through the window by people outside. It's possible the owner may have placed the poster there to scare off would-be intruders, but the strange apparition only piqued peoples' curiosity and helped spread a ghost story.

Nonetheless, rumors of ghosts in the house continued, and the legend was that if you could stay all night in the house, an unknown benefactor would pay you $500 for your bravery. The current owner, Glenn Litton, believes that the previous owner spread the story to keep people away from the house when he wasn't there.

Disappointed in the handy explanation of the ghostly female figure, I continued to ask around and was told a "real" ghost story by Scott Sexton, a local resident. In the 1960s, Sexton and a group of young friends decided to try their courage and spend the night at this abandoned house. Reported to be haunted, the Logan house was a perfect test of bravery for the young boys. The story was that at midnight you would see a woman walking through the house. The boys were scared but determined to be brave. Everyone in the community had told them stories about this house. So they packed snacks, flashlights, sleeping bags, and a radio and sneaked into the house.

Not long after midnight, they began to hear pacing footsteps upstairs. It sounded like several people walking upstairs, although they were the only ones present in the house. Outside, the wind picked up. Suddenly, the front door, which they had left open as an escape route, blew shut with a firm bang. Hearts pounding, the boys were trapped inside with the ghosts. They had brought a radio with them for company, but it stopped playing. Above the sounds of their heartbeats, all of the boys heard a baby crying, and then they distinctly heard someone screaming, "hush." Courage lost, the young boys leapt as one out a front window and ran for home. The next day, their parents escorted the frightened boys to the old Logan house to recover their abandoned belongings. Even now, these grown men wouldn't dream of trying to spend the night in the old house (Sexton, 2004; Litton, 2003; VDHL 95-501).

Saint of Shortsville

Many years ago, a much-loved person in the Shortsville community named Janey Thompson passed away suddenly. Many folks had called Mrs. Thompson a saint since she did so many good deeds for friends and neighbors. The tightly knit community was heartbroken over her death. As was the custom, her body was left upstairs in a bedroom of her house for preparation and bathing for the wake that night. John Wesley, an 18-year old boy in the community, heard that Mrs. Thompson had died. Wesley rushed through his chores, including milking the cows, so later that night he could attend the wake for Mrs. Thompson. By the time he finished, Wesley began to hurry down the dirt road to her house in the approaching dark. As he grew closer to the house, he heard a choir singing and a deep voice reading scripture. The boy walked more quickly to the Thompson house, afraid he had missed the service.

When he neared the house, Wesley saw an upstairs bedroom window open and the white curtains billowing out. Wesley rushed into the house and apologized to the crowd for missing the wake and service. Although the neighbors looked at him strangely, he mentioned that he had heard the singing and the preaching, and it had sounded fine. The mourners just stared at him. One of them told Wesley that the wake hadn't even started yet and there hadn't been any singing or preaching. Chills ran up Wesley's spine when he realized there was no explanation for the sounds he knew he had heard. Perhaps Janey Thompson was enjoying her own personal homecoming into heaven a bit earlier than her earthly service was held (Williams, 2003).

Ch.7 Ghosts and Mysteries of Glade Spring

The small communities of Glade Spring and Emory have their own stories and legends. From murdered slaves, headless horsemen, to hidden Civil War treasures, a visit to these parts is sure to be exciting.

Background on Glade Spring

Glade Spring has a long and fascinating history, dating back to a Native American camp near the town's site. The name of the town comes from the nearby glade with many springs. According to early records, near the town is a field where Native American tribes held a type of Olympics in the fall, with athletic competitions, dancing and socializing. The Porterfield family, who arrived about 1760, was one of the earliest permanent settlers. For many years, Glade Spring was a small, quiet village, but this changed when the railroad was connected in the 1850s. The Civil War slowed down its growth, and local men made up a military unit called The Glade Spring Rifles.

Federal and Confederate troops passed through the town several times, and a cannon emplacements can still be seen just outside Glade Spring on the road to Saltville. After the war, the railroad access made the town into a prime shipping yard for produce, livestock and other local goods. Virginia Intermont College was located in Glade from 1884 to 1892, when it moved to the present location near Bristol. Famous native sons include General Grumble Jones, a Civil War general, and Robert Porterfield, the founder of the Barter Theatre. After the train service discontinued, the growth in the town slowed down, and today, it's a peaceful home to small businesses and residences (Williams 1998).

Greenway Stagecoach Inn

Although it is no longer standing, the Greenway Stagecoach Inn was home to the ghost of a slave boy, mistreated by a callous lodger.

At one time, many inns and taverns were located in this area, mainly along the main transportation route, the old Wilderness Trail. Since this region was the last town on the long journey to Kentucky and beyond, many travelers would stop for food and drink and stay in the inns and taverns. Most of these buildings are now gone.

A large stagecoach inn was once located about five miles east of Abingdon on the Lee Highway along Hog Thief Creek. Built by a man named Greenway in 1790, the large inn was a busy stop on the Wilderness Road. The inn may have originally been constructed of logs, and these were visible under the weather boarding when the inn was still standing. Greenway kept slaves to help run the inn. The young male slaves cared for the many horses in the inn's stables, and the young female slaves helped with housework and cleaning the rooms in the inn. Legend has it that one cold night, a gentleman stopped at the inn, and curtly ordered the stable boy to care for his horse. The weary traveler didn't think to warn the unfortunate boy that his spirited steed was dangerous. When he was trying to lead the horse into the stall, the horse trampled the poor slave to death. Legend says that on cold winter nights, the poor slave boy comes back to the inn to look for the stranger and seek revenge for his death.

The old inn become dilapidated over the years and was torn down at some point in history. Unfortunately, few examples of these early inns remain in the county (Levenson, August 9, 1959).

Sojourn at Washington Springs Hotel

This historic hotel no longer stands near Glade Spring, but locals still tell stories about the once grand hotel. The three story hotel was built with 20 rooms in the mid 1800s by Dr. Edmund Longley. Dr. Longley suffered from physical ailments and the springs helped his health problems. So, he decided to promote the springs and create a resort. Longley taught at Emory and Henry College for many years.

In this time period, folks thought mineral springs were the antidote to many health problems, and resorts were built at these locations all over the nation. Because of the many springs in this region, a number of mineral springs resorts were developed. Washington

Washington Springs Hotel, built in mid-1800s (Courtesy of Historical Society of Washington County, Virginia)

Springs advertised four springs with salubrious properties: Sulphur Springs, Magnesia Soda Iron Springs, Alum Springs, and Leech's Chalybeate Springs. The doctor advertised that these mineral waters could remedy many chronic ailments, including indigestion, liver trouble, rheumatism, dyspepsia (indigestion), and impurities of the blood. Dr. Longley installed a swimming pool, tennis courts, bowling alley, dance pavilion and croquet lawns to attract and entertain the wealthy visitors. The pool was later closed because of copperhead snakes frequenting the pool and the difficulty of keeping it sanitary.

The legend about the health resort is frightening, and it likely scared off many visitors to the resort. A headless man was often seen along the road around Washington Springs. Guests often came back from relaxing walks in terror and babbling stories about a headless man.

Advertisements for the springs brag about their fresh foods (grown in their own gardens), locally grown meat and dairy products. The resort was a social center for the community as well, with weekly dances and music concerts. The resort became popular and was usually full during the summer. Reportedly, guests visited from as far away as China. The owners added a section to the hotel about 1900, bringing it to a total of 46 rooms. The building was expensive to maintain and repair and the business began to decline. Washington Springs resort closed in the 1940s. The hotel became more dilapidated over time and burned down in 1956 (Levenson 1959; Historical Society of Washington County, Virginia 1968).

Woodburn

Mysterious stories are numerous about this Greek Revival style brick house located in Glade Springs on Old Saltville Road. Today, its dilapidated, gray appearance certainly makes them credible.

William Byars had this stately brick home built in 1856 for his nephew, William Byars. The Byars family also built Brook Hall, Cave Springs, and other brick homes in the area. The land originally belonged to Capt. David Beattie and in 1842, included several dwelling houses and 335 acres of land with many water springs.

Sarah Taylor Byars, the wife of William Byars, was known as a thrifty and efficient homemaker. An intelligent woman, Mrs. Byars instructed the slaves to bury the family silver in the garden during the Civil War. The Yankee troops passed by the house without finding the treasure. Luckily, the silver was recovered after the war, and the

Woodburn, built in 1856

descendents of the family have passed it down through generations.

The household also had part of the cellar closed up as a hiding place during the Civil War and buried the farm's tobacco crop in the subflooring of the attic. It's interesting that there are several stories in the county about hiding tobacco crops from the Yankees, proof that tobacco was king here. Legend has it that the cellar also housed a whipping post, but it has since been removed. Today, the stately historic house sits abandoned and in need of renovation. Hopefully, a buyer will purchase the home and be able to restore it to its former glory. Who knows? Part of the silver treasure may remain buried on the property (Levenson 1958; King 1994:160; VDHL 95-436).

Hidden Yankee Treasure near Glade Spring

During the Civil war, a group of Confederate soldiers managed to steal a large amount of money, reportedly over a million dollars, from the Union army. The Union soldiers then chased the Confederates along the road from Glade Springs to Saltville. The Confederates, sensing imminent capture, decided the best thing to do would be to hide the money.

Rumor has it they located a cave and hid the money in it and later blew up the entrance to the cave to hide it. Unfortunately, the limestone topography in this region produced many caves, and nobody knew the exact location of the hidden money. The stolen Yankee money has never been found and may still be hidden deep within a cave somewhere between Glade Spring and Saltville. (Williams 1998).

Ebbing Springs or Old Glade Church

The old cemetery lies peacefully under old trees behind the white frame church near Glade Spring. It clearly has a story to tell, one rooted in the Presbyterians, the earliest congregations in the region. The large numbers of Ulster Irish settlers bequeathed a legacy of Presbyterian worship to Washington County. Prior to 1772, two Presbyterian congregations were active: one at Sinking Spring in Abingdon and one at Ebbing Springs, in old Glade Springs. The

Ebbing Springs or the Old Glade Church, built in 1845

Reverend Charles Cummings, the famous "Fighting Parson," served both congregations for a time. The first church for Ebbing Springs, a log building, was built at the site in 1795, and the present brick church was built in 1845. Reportedly, this site was also the original location of Fort Kincannon, built for protection against Native Americans.

The section closest to the churchyard is the oldest part of the graveyard. Many inscriptions on the markers have faded away through time. Tradition maintains that the oldest burial is a child's grave with an iron marker bearing the initials "M.H.", a Kincannon child killed by Indians in 1800.

The adjacent cemetery was the final resting place for many early settlers, such as the Beatties, Kincannons, Byars, Clarks, and Robinsons, as well as well-known persons. Dr. William L. Dunn, a surgeon with Mosby's Rangers and Judge John A. Buchanan, Justice of the State Supreme Court, are well-known heroes who contributed to the local community and the larger world. Perhaps the most famous of the cemetery residents is General William E. "Grumble" Jones, a Confederate leader and hero. Today, many of the descendents of the early congregation worship at the church and keep the cemetery well-maintained (VDHL 95-0135; Summers 1989:138-139, 341, 371)

Historic Photograph of Brook Hall in disrepair (Courtesy of Historical Society of Washington County, Virginia)

Brook Hall today, after extensive renovations

Brook Hall

Brook Hall is one of the oldest houses in the area and has seen a fair share of history from its position on the old Wagon Road. Several ghost stories surround the mysterious house and its once extensive lands.

This imposing brick structure sits grandly on a hill on U.S. Rt. 11, the old Wagon Road. The original Brook Hall was a log house built in 1773-1774 located north of the present brick home. This early log home was an early inn and store.

Colonel William Byars, a wealthy landholder in southwest Virginia, completed the existing Brook Hall about 1826. Col. Byars hired English cabinet-makers to complete much of the beautiful woodwork, and no expense was spared in its decoration. The house was designed with 27 rooms. As a large landowner, Col. Byars owned slaves to manage his land and estate. The slave quarters were located in the back of the house. After the Civil War, the family gave their freed slaves land from their estate and money to build a community, now known as Blacksburg.

Col. Byars was one of the founders of Emory and Henry College and served as a justice in Washington County. Byars was a major and

Original Brookhall log cabin, built 1773-1774 (Courtesy of Historical Society of Washington County, Virginia)

later colonel in the War of 1812. Byars was also a farmer, and owned a mill, a distillery, and a general store on Cedar Creek. Reportedly, President Andrew Jackson was a guest in the house during his travels through Virginia to Tennessee.

With such a rich history, stories about the house were sure to develop and be passed on through generations. Eleanor Williams tells a story that happened before the Civil War. According to the story, a small 6-year-old slave named Jezzia once lived at Brook Hall. One cold winter's night, Col. Byars instructed his son to bring in a newborn lamb. Instead, Col. Byars' son demanded that small Jezzia bring in the lamb for him. Jezzia's mother protested, "But he has no shoes or coat." Col. Byars' son replied, "It makes no difference to me. The lamb needs to be brought in." So, poor Jezzia was sent out in the winter night with neither shoes nor a coat. By the time the slave boy found the lamb, it had died. Cold and afraid, Jezzia returned to the Hall. In a fit of irrational rage, Col. Byars' son took Jezzia to the springhouse and beat him. Sadly, Jezzia died, and the cruel son left his body there. Jezzia's mother went looking for him and found him dead in the springhouse. The slaves carried him back to the slave quarters, but they couldn't bury him because of the frozen ground. In those days, bodies would have to be stored through the winter in an outbuilding until the spring thaw allowed the families to dig a grave.

The cruelty of Mr. Byars must have created an unsettled spirit. On cold, winter nights, several people on the Brook Hall grounds have heard a boy's screams for mercy coming from the location of the springhouse. Many locals avoid the property at night, especially during the winter. Injustice and violence can create apparitions that remain at the scene of their deaths.

Although Col. Byars was a wealthy man, he was also careful with his money. During the Civil War, both the Home Guard and the Union Army appropriated livestock, food and money for their respective causes. Col. Byars was determined to protect his money, much of it in gold bars brought from England. In 1862, he and two slaves transported his treasure of a million dollars by wagon to a hidden location. These two slaves were sold the next day and sent to New Orleans. The secret of the location of the gold died with Col. Byars, who never revealed the location of the money. The treasure's location has never been found.

Another story commonly told about Brook Hall is that an Emory and Henry College student stopped one night to get a cold drink of water at the springhouse. His body was found the next morning with his throat cut. His murder was never solved (Williams, 2003; VDHL 95-04, Historical Society of Washington County Bulletin 1968).

Beattie House Hidden Treasure

The existing brick home was built on this property just east of Emory in 1853. John Beattie and Ellen Gilmore Beattie purchased this rich bottomland in 1783. The Beattie family was among the earliest settlers and major landowners in the Glade Spring area. The Beatties were active in local government and in church life. The couple first built a log home on the land and raised a family. One of their sons, David Beattie, was a captain in the famed Battle of King's Mountain, while another son, John, died in this battle. Madison Beattie, grandson of John and Ellen, inherited the land from his father, William, and he had a brick house built. Unfortunately, the house burned to the ground on the day in 1853 that it was finished. Reportedly, Madison began construction of the present two-story brick house the next day on the same site.

Legends about this house are numerous, but the most fascinating story took place during the Civil War. According to Levenson's newspaper article, during the Civil War, Madison Beattie instructed the most trusted family slave to take the family silver and money and bury it in a hidden location. Nobody knew exactly where it was buried, but the slave was seen taking the treasure down toward the creek behind the house. The Union soldiers did arrive in the area as feared. The slaves were installing a roof on a log outbuilding and became frightened at the army's arrival. Unfortunately, one of the large logs fell and killed the slave who had hidden the family valuables. Beattie didn't learn of the money's location before the slave died. The secret of the location of the family treasure died along with the unlucky slave. The silver and the money have never been found. Legend has it that the treasure is located somewhere on the farm property, although attempts to find it have been unsuccessful (Levenson March 15, 1959; VDHL 95-0443).

Beattie House, built 1853

Ch. 8 Ghosts of Emory and Henry College

History of Emory and Henry College

Emory and Henry College, located in the small community of Emory, was established in 1838 and is one of the oldest colleges in southwest Virginia. The college is affiliated with the United Methodist Church and is consistently ranked highly in Virginia college listings. The surrounding farm land developed into a village because of the college. The lovely 168 acres campus is also unique because the entire campus is listed on the National Register of Historic Places and on the Virginia Register of Historic Landmarks. The college community takes pride in being a small, closely-knit, private liberal arts college. J.E.B. Stuart, a leading Confederate general, was probably the most famous student from the college.

Although the campus appears serene, the college has a long history of ghost tales. Some students admit to being scared to venture into certain buildings or areas of campus after dark. Ghost stories are common on college campuses and serve many purposes, most impor-

Tobias Smyth Cabin, built about 1789 was moved to the campus

tantly, to create a common bond between strangers in an unknown environment (Stevenson 1963:1-16).

Green Slippers in the Tobias Smyth Cabin

The Tobias Smyth cabin, which dates to about 1789, is now located on the Emory and Henry college campus, but originally was located a mile north of the school on the North Fork of the Holston River. Tobias Smyth was one of the founders of the college.

At first glance, the cabin seems quiet and peaceful. However, stories of ghosts surround the cabin. The Smyth family often had their young niece, Melissa, stay with them to visit. Mrs. Smyth made her a special pair of green satin slippers to wear in the house. One night when the Smyths went to chapel, Melissa was too sick to attend. As a precaution, they left her safely locked inside the cabin. But, when they returned from church, the front door stood open, and Melissa was missing. The Smyths searched the cabin, but only found one green slipper inside and the other one in the yard. Mr. and Mrs. Smyth were both distraught with grief at their niece's disappearance and searched the area for days. Many neighbors believed that renegade federal soldiers abducted her and killer her. The confederate troops caught a group of these Union soldiers near Wytheville, but none of them confessed to killing the child. Mrs. Smyth was particularly heartbroken about Melissa, and she laid out her pretty green slippers neatly in her bedroom as if waiting for her to return. It is said that if you sit quietly through the night in the cabin, that you can see a small girl, clad in a white nightgown and carrying a candle. Melissa returns to search for her beloved green satin slippers (Leidig, 2003)

Murdered Yankees in Wiley Hall

During October 1864, a Civil War battle occurred in nearby Saltville. Saltville was the source of the important salt mines and was a strategic objective of the Union army. Under General Stoneman, the federal calvary led a raid through southwest Virginia from Bristol to destroy and block the salt supplies of the Confederacy. At Saltville, General Breckenridge led the Confederate troops. The Union forces

Wiley Hall, used as Civil War hospital (Courtesy Emory & Henry Archives.)

engaged with the Confederate soldiers near Max Meadow, and the Union forces were defeated. The injured Union soldiers were taken prisoner and housed with the wounded Confederate soldiers in Wiley Hall. Wiley Hall, on the campus of Emory and Henry, served as a hospital during this time and contained about 350 beds. The third and fourth floors and the garret of the hall were used to accommodate some 150-200 wounded Union soldiers. The Union troops included some African-American soldiers from the Fifth United States Colored Calvary. Wiley Hall became the stage for a cowardly act of violence.

About five days after the battle, three unknown men entered Wiley Hall and killed several of the African-American prisoners in their sick beds. The next day, an armed band of Confederate rangers, led by Captain Champ Ferguson, took over the hospital. Champ Ferguson was a guerilla Confederate soldier who often took the law into his own hands. Ferguson and his men were searching for

Lieutenant E.C. Smith of the Thirteenth Kentucky Calvary. Supposedly, Ferguson was planning to avenge the mistreatment of his family by Lt. Smith. Ferguson's ire stemmed from an incident in which Lt. Smith had forced Ferguson's wife to undress and march naked down a public road. Another story is that Lt. Smith had captured or killed some of Ferguson's men.

Ferguson located the injured Smith in his hospital bed at Wiley Hall. He approached Smith's bed and sat down. According to Sensing, Champ patted the gun in his hand and said, "Smith, do you see this? Well, I'm going to kill you." Smith raised his head and said, "Champ, for God's sake, don't shoot me here." (Sensing 1942:182). Ferguson then put the gun to Smith's head and shot him in cold blood. The Confederate hospital doctors arrived at the murder scene and tried to arrest Ferguson. One of the doctors, Major W.W. Stringfield, threatened to shoot Ferguson if he killed any other patients. The guerilla captain left the hospital but promised to return and murder the remaining Yankees. Ferguson was later arrested and court-martialed. He was tried in Nashville, Tennessee in 1865 and found guilty of approximately 50 murder charges and war crimes. He was one of only two Confederate officers who were convicted of war crimes from the Civil War. Champ Ferguson was hanged by the neck on October 20, 1865.

However, the story doesn't end there. Supposedly, Ferguson became friendly with the executioner and was seen shaking hands just before the hanging. Ferguson only hanged for a short time, and then his wife and daughter came with a wagon to collect his body. Many believed he may have survived the "abbreviated" hanging, and that his family smuggled him away. He has a tombstone in White County, Tennessee near his home place. However, his family immediately left for the west after this, and Ferguson may have gone on to establish a quiet life in the new territory.

The bloodstains on the floor and bullet holes on the walls remained in Wiley Hall. Students later told stories about mysterious moanings, lights turned off and on, and ghostly soldier apparitions in the building. Some students saw a wounded soldier leaning against the wall, who didn't seem to threaten anyone, just disappeared. An exterior light hanging on the building would sometimes swing gently when nobody was moving it and the wind was quiet. Wiley Hall later became outmoded and was demolished in 1912 to construct the new Administration building. (Stevenson 1963: 93-95; Sensing 1942: 177-180).

New Wiley Hall

More than any other building on campus, the new Wiley Hall, the Administration Building, seems to have its fair share of ghosts. Several witnesses have seen a dark shadow floating through the basement of the building. Students and faculty claim that a female ghost nicknamed Freda moves items around, opens and closes doors, and carries a lantern down the halls. Another reported sighting is of a strange young woman dressed in white. Campus security guards saw the woman trying desperately to open several doors on the outside of the building. As the officers came closer to the girl, she disappeared through the doors (Sykes 2003; Aird 2003).

Memorial Chapel

Memorial Chapel, built in 1956

Memorial Chapel is a beautiful campus chapel which was completed in 1956. The chapel is a favorite location for weddings and is booked up years in advance. Although it is picturesque, there is another side to the chapel. Some people have reported seeing a young woman, who has been named Clara, sitting beside one of the stained glass windows in the chapel. For some reason, she is seen just after a new fallen snow. Those who have seen Clara mention the smell of roses near where she was seen, although no such flowers were located nearby (Sykes 2003).

Wiley Jackson Dormitory

Wiley Jackson is a girl's dormitory on campus. Students tell several stories about strange happenings in the building. Supposedly, a college student committed suicide in the third floor bathroom. Distraught over being stood up for a date, the girl hanged herself on a showerhead in the middle stall. Residents have told stories about the water in that particular shower suddenly spraying out of control, while the other showerheads remain normal. Also, footsteps can be heard pacing up and down the halls, leading students to believe that it's the sad girl still waiting for her date.

Another story deals with Satan worshippers in the dorm. In the 1980s a group of females were thought to practice Satanism and witchcraft in their dorm rooms. Many students have seen the figure of Satan in the dorm and have heard evil satanic chanting (DeHart, 2004; Sykes 2003; Aird 2003).

Byars Building

Stories are plentiful about the Byars fine arts building. By day, a graceful building housing the theatre and music departments, at night it becomes a different place entirely. Lovely paintings assume a ghostly appearance and pianos play by themselves. Some have heard footsteps in the basement. It's also reported that a suspended light fixture on the ceiling of the front porch swings gently on dark, windless nights. The story is that someone pushed a student from the window and he tried to grasp the lantern to break his fall. However, the young man died from the fall, and many believe his spirit causes the lantern to swing on dark nights (Aird 2003).

Emory Cemetery

The historic cemetery was established in 1847, but no official records of the grounds remain. Several of the headstones have weathered and are illegible. The cemetery is quite old and is the resting place for Civil War soldiers who died at the college when it served as a hospital. Lined up in neat rows, almost 200 Confederate soldier graves from the Civil War battle at nearby Saltville are grim reminders of this terrible war. A small number of Union soldiers were also buried here, but were later moved to another cemetery. Sightings of strange phenomena include a light that approaches along the railroad tracks and then climbs the cemetery hill and then disappears. A student once saw a Confederate soldier in full uniform marching up the hill toward the graveyard. Most people avoid the cemetery after dark. Several folks have reported hearing footsteps walking behind them.

The campus security chief regularly patrols the historic Emory cemetery located just across the railroad tracks from campus. Students sometimes hang out at the old cemetery and may cause mischief. About 2 am on a rainy, foggy night, Mr. Brown drove his car around the cemetery. All seemed quiet. After he turned his car around in the horseshoe turn, the fog suddenly changed in color to blood red. The thick fog surrounded his car and glowed red in the headlights. This strange occurrence chilled Mr. Brown, so he took it as a warning. He quickly drove his car down the hill and out of the cemetery. Another strange apparition reported near the cemetery is a floating lantern. The person carrying the light hasn't ever been seen.

Another story about the cemetery is that young female college students who dabbled in Satanism would burn crosses at the cemetery. During a ceremony one dark night, a cross suddenly exploded into flames for no apparent reason. Frightened at this strange event, the girls fled from the cemetery (Brown 2004 and Aird 2003).

Waterhouse Hall

The college students have spread the tale of "Nora" of Waterhouse Hall for many years. The story goes that a young black maid, Nora, became pregnant with the child of either the church bishop or college president, depending on the story's source. Supposedly, the bishop killed Nora by pushing her down the stairs. Another version of this story is that Nora died during childbirth. A group of students reported contacting Nora through a Ouija board. Sightings of Nora and other eerie happenings have been reported on the second floor of the building. Fortunately, Nora seems peaceful and merely shuts and locks doors and opens windows. Others have heard sounds of her crying. Nora is also blamed for rearranging things in the buildings, perhaps a throwback to her days as a maid (Sykes 2003; Aird 2003; Willis 2003).

Kilmakronen, originally built in 1776

Ch. 9 Fascinating Washington County Houses and Characters

"Fort Kilmakronen"

Built in 1776, Fort Kilmakronen (or Kilmackronen) is one of the most fascinating houses in Washington County. The historic stone house has a rich history, and several intriguing stories have been recorded about the house and lands. Any resident or visitor to the area should know some of its history to appreciate its legends. From Native Americans to Tory spies to lost graveyards, the plantation provides a tapestry of tales. The mysterious Ebbing Spring also is a unique element of the farm complex.

The plantation was one of the earliest surveys made by John Buchanan on the Holston River and was recorded in 1746 with 2600 acres along the Middle Fork of the Holston. It has historically been known as a fort, but it is unclear if it was built or used for that purpose. Most historians don't believe that it was built as a fort, but somehow the term was linked to the building.

At the time of construction of the house, the owners noted remnants of a fortified Native American village. The property was also called Indian Fields. Some stones from the Native American embankments are said to have been used in building the stone walls. Past property owners found a burial ground for the Native Americans near the house site, but over the years, it was plowed over and destroyed. To date, property owners have recovered many Native American artifacts from the fields, including tools such as hammerstones, and points, as well as pieces of pottery.

Col. Patton named the property for his ancestral home, "Kilmacrennan" in Donegal, Ireland. Captain James Thompson later acquired the property, and, according to some accounts, built the structure to be a fort, with a surrounding stockade. The original house was built with two stories, 60 by 30 feet, and limestone walls three feet thick. The house is unusual because it was one of the few stone houses built in the area. It would be the only stone fort in southwest Virginia and the only fort still remaining from the pioneer days. Regardless of its original use or later use, the building and farm are significant in early settlement in the area.

Captain Thompson was a wealthy and important leader in the early settlement days. He married Catharine Shelby, daughter of General Evan Shelby. In May of 1771, he was constable for the Holston section of Botetourt County. He was also captain of the Indian rangers and militia, serving in the Indian wars and during the Revolutionary War (Levenson July 19, 1959; Summers 1989: 22, 274; Historical Society of Washington County 1968; Aronhime October 27, 1963; VDHL 95-10).

Old Ebbing Spring Meeting House

If memories from old churches and graveyards lingered on the landscape, then the Kilmakronen property would be full to bursting. The first Ebbing Spring Meeting House was built near the middle fork of the Holston on the Kilmakronen tract, about a mile from the main house. The log church measured approximately 80-100 feet long and was 40 feet wide, but nothing remains of the building today.

Ebbing Spring Meeting House site and burying ground

An old graveyard near the Meeting House is the final resting place for approximately 30-40 early pioneers. The congregation used the meeting house until the 1920s. Sadly, now the graves are unmarked, and identities and their exact locations have been lost.

During the historic survey conducted by Vivian Coletti in 1993, one tombstone dated 1771 was still left at the site with the name "Peleg Cole." A monument erected by the Ebbing Spring Presbyterian Church is located about 300 feet south of the marker. A stone foundation remaining from the David Stump log house is also near the church site.

Below the church and graveyard site is the Ebbing Spring, from which the community derived its name. The peaceful spring rises and falls about 7 to 8 inches in depth every 15 minutes. You can watch a large rock be covered and then emerge from the cool water. It's believed that a large stone underground acts as a dam which fills and then spills out above ground (VDHL 95-0010; Johnson 2004).

Tory Spy and Swift Justice near Kilmakronen

Stories of captured British spies in the region are not that uncommon, but this particular story has its own charm. During the Revolutionary War, many spies for the British were present in the

Site of Capture and Execution of Tory Spy

area, relaying messages between the British and the Native Americans living nearby. Neighbors didn't trust each other, and tension was high.

John Broady, the manservant of Colonel William Campbell, told this story many years ago. Broady had been born into slavery in the Campbell family and showing a sharp mind, was sent to school with his childhood friend and future master, William Campbell. In 1793, Campbell gave Broady his freedom for serving him faithfully through the Revolutionary War.

One day in 1780, Colonel William Campbell was returning from church at Ebbing Springs Meeting House with some friends and his family. The meeting house was located on the Kilmakronen tract about a mile from the house. The group noticed a man from about a hundred yards away, who upon seeing them, turned off the road and galloped off on his horse into the woods. Figuring that this behavior could show the man was up to no good, Campbell handed his baby, Sally Buchanan Campbell to John Broady. Mrs. Campbell was afraid that Broady would be needed, so she took the baby and sent the servant after his master. Campbell, followed by John Broady, chased the man on horseback across the ford of the Middle Fork. Campbell caught up with him, threw his pistols into the river and used the man's own sword to capture the man. Luckily, several of Campbell's neighbors, James Fullen, Edward Farris and William Bates, had come upon the group and offered help. The men recognized the man as Francis Hopkins, who was once a hired hand for Colonel Campbell and was known as a Tory spy and horse thief in the area. Hopkins, who had been arrested in 1778 and in June, 1779, had broken out of a jail west of the settlement of Abingdon. He was guilty of carrying papers that detailed the settlers who agreed to enlist to fight with the British against the colony. Several of the men listed as British sympathizers were located by Col. Campbell but later tried and freed. Hopkins' accomplices were later found to have been hiding in a cave along the Holston, but they fled before being captured.

The group of neighbors agreed the spy should be hanged at the site of the river ford. Francis Hopkins confessed his crimes, and they hanged him on a sycamore tree near the ford of the river. The halter from the spy's horse was fastened to a tree limb and the other end to his neck. The horse was then led out from under him, leaving the spy to hang. Years later, a property owner found a human jawbone on the ground's surface near this site under the sycamore tree. The jawbone may have been from the shallow grave of Hopkins. There were many eerie stories about this site passed down through the family and the family slaves. Nobody lingers near the Tory Ford after dark.

Col. Campbell was no stranger to meting out justice to Tory spies, since in 1777 he had captured a spy carrying papers hidden in the soles of his shoes. Campbell and his friends were able to obtain a confession, and they hanged this spy from a nearby tree (Summers 1989:272-277; Aronhime October 27, 1963).

Kirk-Meek Stone House

Located off the Lee Highway near Chilhowie, an old stone house sits peacefully in a pasture. This unique stone house was built at this site between 1772 and 1787, according to the state historic survey. It is the earliest stone house remaining in Washington County, and for

Kirk-Meek stone house and store, built between 1772 and 1787

that reason, it has been included in these stories of the past. Many stories of interesting events at the house have been passed down through the years.

According to Huff, the stones for the house were quarried from the limestone rocks around the nearby large spring and hauled to the building site by ox-drawn sleds. John Kirk was the owner when it was built. Local historians believe the some stonemason who built nearby Kilmakronen likely built this house also. Oral tradition tells that Hessian soldiers in the area during the American Revolution built these types of stone buildings.

The original structure was a large house for that time period, likely measuring 96 feet in length. Today, only a small portion of the original building remains. The house has a rich history, once serving as a center for barter and trade. A store was located in the building, which was a stopping place for traders, peddlers, covered wagons on the journey to the west, and stagecoaches. As a community center, political rallies and speeches were held there, as well as circuses and other traveling shows. The location of the Kirk-Meek house is along the old stage road leading from the Town House to Black's Fort (now Abingdon).

One unique story from the nineteenth century heyday of the store concerns a traveling circus. As the circus was packing up after a show, one of the wagons turned over. The wagon contained the bag with all of the money the circus had taken in during that show. "Helpful" neighbors assisted in righting the wagon and making it ready for travel. As they left, the circus crew checked for the money and found that it had disappeared during the accident. Nobody knew who took the money, and it was never recovered.

In 1831, a particularly notable political gathering occurred at Meek's store when Joseph Draper of Wythe County and Charles Johnston of Washington County were scheduled for a debate. Mr. Johnston couldn't appear, so a substitute was found who had been summering at Chilhowie Sulphur Springs. Senator William C. Preston, of South Carolina, who was grandnephew of Patrick Henry, and grandson of General William Campbell, volunteered to champion Charles Johnston. Senator Preston was considered one of the greatest speakers of the U.S. Senate. Senator Preston's famous speech was quoted and discussed in southwest Virginia for many years afterwards.

The historic stone homestead also was the birthplace of one of the most fascinating characters of Virginia and the west, known as the "Davie Crockett of the Northwest." Joseph L. Meek, who later became first U.S. marshal and sheriff of the Oregon territory and well-known Rocky Mountain hunter, trapper and Indian fighter, was reared in this house. Joseph Meek was born in 1810 in the stone house. Meek also was a friend of Kit Carson and his wild adventures reportedly eclipsed any of Carson's.

When only a raw boy of 18 or so years, Joseph decided to find adventure away from home. He neglected to tell his parents of his plans, but "stowed away" on a westward-bound wagon train which had stopped at the family store. When the occupants of the wagon discovered him in Abingdon, several hours journey away, they allowed him to join the wagon group for their adventures out west. The brave lad traveled from Louisville to St. Louis and then joined a fur company headed for the Rocky Mountains. Meek prospered in this new territory and was instrumental in gaining statehood for Oregon. A biographer of Joseph Meek commented that he was one of the great figures in the history of the western United States. It seems odd that a curious boy's stowing away in a wagon turned into a grand adventure in the early days of our nation (Huff, 2004; Wilson 1932; VDHL 95-26; Victor 1983:1-40; Vestal 1952).

Lewis Smith Tavern

Only parts of the foundation remain of Smith's Tavern, just in front of the Kirk-Meek stone house. It served as a boarding house up until the mid 1800s and was destroyed by a fire. It too has a story to tell. The current white frame house was built in the early 1900s on the old foundation and using old chimneys. An amusing story about the white frame house concerns two young men who stayed there many years ago. The two young men departed early the next morning to walk up to Whitetop Mountain. It turns out that one of the young men was none other than Theodore Roosevelt, who was visiting his sister, Eleanor, as she attended the Whitetop Music Festival (VDHL 95-468; Huff, 2004).

Indian Fields Stone and Log House

Located just outside Chilhowie, this unique house with a cantilevered second story is one of the most unusual in the area. The mystery of its original function still hasn't been solved. The cantilever style is found in barns in this area, but rarely is found in houses. Indian Fields was likely built about 1790 and was part of the original extensive Indian Fields tract. Vivian Coletti, the current property owner, believes the log and stone house was used as a neighborhood fort in the early settlement days. In fact, some evidence suggests that it may be the Fort Thompson referred to in early records.

According to Ms. Coletti, the structure wasn't built as a single family home, because the three pens or living areas were not originally connected and could only be accessed by the exterior porch. The unique architectural style is described by Coletti as mid-European with Germanic building techniques. The first level is made of lime-

Indian Fields cantilevered stone house, built about 1790

stone and the second and one-half story levels are constructed of V-notched logs. The second and one-half story are cantilevered with a galleried overbay or porch. The four interior fireplaces are very large and imposing, measuring as large as 4'6" high, 2' deep and 7'2" wide. Coletti reports the holders for cranes and pot niches are still present in the kitchen fireplace. A faint road trace in front of the house leading to the Middle Fork of the Holston River nearby may be the remnants of the original wagon trail.

This building is located on the original Indian Fields tract. This tract was surveyed for Colonel James Patton in 1746 and included 2600 acres. Col. James Thompson, grandson of Co. Patton, who also owned the Town House in Chilhowie, was the next owner. Through the years it became dilapidated and was used as a tenant house. The current owners, Vivian and Benny Coletti, have carefully restored much of it and renovated it for modern use.

The original function of this house remains a mystery, but the structure was likely a neighborhood fort, possibly Fort Thompson. The unique architectural design and its integrity certainly make it one of the most interesting houses remaining from the early settlement days in the area (Coletti 2004; VDHL 95-48).

Town House

Although only a few large chimneys remain on the site, the Town House was one of the earliest buildings in the area. Few residents realize the significant role the house once played in the region. Today, a restaurant in Chilhowie, "the Town House Grill," is named for the house.

Only chimneys remain of the famous Town House, near Chilhowie (Courtesy of Paul Pendell)

The site is located on a hill at the intersection of U.S. 11 and Sulphur Springs Road, just inside the town of Chilhowie. Only portions of the tall rock chimneys remain surrounded by only a few remaining ancient oaks. A lone stone marker bears witness that an early building and neighborhood fort stood here. At the bottom of the hill is a spring which served as a water source for the early occupants of the house. You only need to squint your eyes to imagine this bottom land in the past, filled with deer, elk, buffalo, and bear.

This site may have been the site of the first building erected in lower southwestern Virginia. Colonel James Patton likely built the log cabin on the site about 1748 when he selected this hill as a good spot for a town. The log building was enlarged over the years, a brick addition constructed, and the weather boarding was added over the logs. Some historians believe this site was the location of the cabin of

Samuel Stalnaker built in 1750, once the most western point of the frontier. The next owners of the house and land were Capt. James Thompson and his wife, who was Col. Patton's daughter. James Thompson (1747-1811), one of the wealthiest men in this area, was magistrate of Botetourt and Fincastle County.

The famous Town House served as a neighborhood fort, a public building and a stagecoach tavern. As a stagecoach relay station, passengers could enter the Town House for rest, food and lodging, and the coach drivers could change the horses. The House was a strategic fort, rather than a fort where settlers gathered for protection. According to some historians, Samuel Stalnaker, an early settler in the area, operated an "ordinary" or tavern in the Town House for many years. In its heyday the Town House is said to have hosted two presidents, Andrew Jackson and James K. Polk. Cock fights held across the old Indian trail, later the stagecoach road, were popular events and customers bet large amounts of money and even parcels of land for entertainment. Revolutionary War and Civil War soldiers

Town House about 1900 (Courtesy Historical Society of Washington County, Virginia)

also used the surrounding land as a mustering and drilling grounds. During Stoneman's raid with Union forces in 1864, Stoneman actually stayed in the Town House for several days. The house was even used later as a Methodist parsonage. The first surveyed road, built on the old Buffalo Trail, in southwest Virginia ran from the Town House west to 18 Mile Creek in Abingdon.

The sturdy house was built of hand-hewn logs with two limestone rock chimneys at either end. The builders used hand wrought iron spikes, square nails and long wooden pins. A large brick detached kitchen stood to the east of the house. The site also contained slave quarters. The interior woodwork, doors, and locks were intricately worked and quite unusual.

The origin of its name is unknown, but Fincastle County records as early as 1773 refer to it as the Town House. Over the years, the old building was vacant, became dilapidated and finally collapsed, leaving only the great stone chimneys as mute witnesses of war councils, tavern brawls, and the political struggles of the new frontier.

Nearby to the Town House was Sulphur Springs, a summer resort popular in its day. Robert Gannaway opened Chilhowie Springs in 1815 and it was quite well known. Even though the springs had a strong sulphur odor, people believed that washing one's hands in the water would cause them to become soft and white again. The springs offered a race track, camping and cabins for lodging. Camp meetings and political rallies were also held at the Sulphur Springs camp as early as 1819 (Aronhime, March 31, 1963; Wilson 1932: 6, 7, 50, 80, 286-288; Cole 1993: 7-11).

John Floyd Elopement

Goodridge Wilson provides a fascinating story of early Chilhowie days in his book about Smyth County. It includes the necessary elements of a good story: danger, love, and intrigue. A handsome young man from Kentucky named John Floyd was at one of the early musters at the Town House. Floyd was the son of John Floyd Sr., a romantic hero of the Revolutionary days. At a celebration for the muster, the younger Floyd could not be located. Folks soon noticed that Letitia Preston, daughter of Col. William Preston, who had came over for the social events after the muster, was also missing. Someone remembered seeing Miss Letitia seated behind Mr. Floyd on his spirited Kentucky horse as it galloped away from the festivities. The couple arrived back from Kentucky as Mr. and Mrs. John Floyd. Floyd later became Governor of Virginia (Wilson 1932: 283-287).

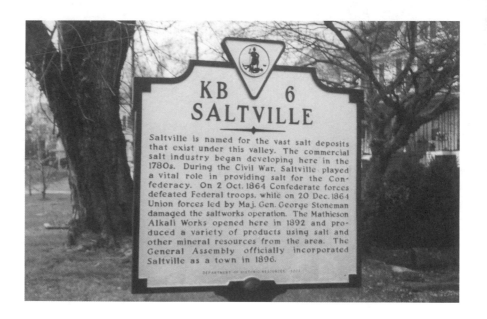

Ch. 10 Spooky Old Saltville and Smyth County

The Saltville area is one of the most unique in this region, due to the presence of underground deposits of salt. Evidence of early Native American occupation has been found in the area, and fossils of mastodons have been discovered near the salt licks. The valley was known very early as "Buffalo Lick" because the animals carved trails into the area to lick the salt. In 1748, Charles Campbell secured the first land patent. Salt manufacturing was the earliest industry here in the late 1700s. A fascinating feature in the valley was a lake which contained salt and fresh water on different sides. Since it supplied the necessary salt for the Confederacy and the region, Saltville was a prime target of the federal forces during the Civil War. The Battle of Sanders Hill occurred in late September 1864, and the Yankees were defeated. But, during General Stoneman's raid in December 1864, the Union troops captured the town and destroyed the salt wells. Fortunately, many of the salt wells had not been discovered, and salt production continued after a few weeks. Several industries developed in the area to take advantage of the natural resources and provided

Steam powered pumps like these pumped the brine from the wells through the log pipes to the salt furnaces.

employment for the local population. However, most of these industries are gone now, and a natural gas facility is the newest industry. An outdoor model of the salt process near the entrance to town shows the early history of this fascinating industry (Kent 1991:15-35).

Conquistadors May Have Visited Saltville in 1567

Jim Glanville published a fascinating investigation in The Smithfield Review that uses primary and secondary sources to show a strong possibility that Spanish conquistadors with the Juan Pardo expedition visited the Chilhowie-Saltville area in 1567.

A Native-American woman named Luisa Menendez gave documented testimony in 1600 about the Chilhowie/Saltville area. The woman married a Spanish soldier when he was exploring the area, and she went with him back to the coast. This woman said she came from "Maniatique," where there were springs of salt water from which the Indians made salt and that this town had more salt water than any other place in the country. The town which she refers to was likely Saltville or Chilhowie. Archeologists studying artifacts and settlement patterns speculate that the Chilhowie-Saltville area was "a salt-powered chiefdom" and a trading center for Native Americans. Unfortunately, because of the salt extraction process and early industrial development, few archeological sites in Saltville remain which might yield archeological evidence to support a Spanish visit to the town (Glanville 2004:70-108).

Madame Russell House

The Madame Russell House seems to have more than its fair share of ghosts, haints, and strange beings. Built of logs in 1788, the original cabin was located behind the Madam Russell Memorial Methodist Church. The original cabin is no longer here, but about 1972 preservationists moved a similar type log cabin to the site. Even though the Madame Russell house is gone, the stories about the house linger on.

Elizabeth Russell, later known as Madame Russell, was a sister to Patrick Henry and a much respected woman in the colonial days here. She first married General William Campbell and after being widowed, married General William Russell. She was known as an intelligent orator and active religious leader. In 1808, a presidential

Log cabin at the site, which is similar to Madame Russell House

candidate named James Madison visited in her home, and he stated he knew no other more eloquent orator. Preferring to ride horseback rather than in a carriage, Madame Russell cut a fine figure in a man's coat and felt hat. She had a long, fulfilling life of 76 years until her death in 1825 and is buried at the Preston Cemetery in Aspenvale.

One story about the house serves as a lesson for children to listen to their parents. In about 1845, the Taylor family lived in the house. Mrs. Taylor left her young daughter and a friend playing in their yard while she went to a neighbor's house. Her instructions were that they could eat only one peach from a basket inside the house. Mrs. Taylor shook her finger and warned the young misses that if they sneaked more than one peach, the silk petticoats from upstairs would come down and get them. Naturally, being young and greedy, the two girls decided to sneak more than one of the delicious peaches. As they reached into the basket, the girls both heard a slight sound. It was the sound of silk petticoats, coming from the head of the stairs. The youngsters abandoned their plan for a second peach and ran away from the house. A safe distance from the house, the girls waited for Mrs. Taylor to return home, but kept the story to themselves.

The Madame Russell house was periodically occupied during the years afterward, often by families who scoffed at the ghost stories. However, the families had their own supernatural encounters and left the house quickly. Occupants didn't stay long in the Madame Russell house. Legend said that nobody would sleep upstairs in the house. Doors inside the house couldn't be kept closed, and even after being locked, would be open in the morning. Folks heard chains jangling across the upstairs floor. With so many stories and bizarre encounters, nobody wanted to live there, and the house was abandoned. Young boys might challenge each other to enter the house at night, but many of them had ghostly encounters that scared them away.

Strange stories circulated about the land surrounding the cabin, too. There were reports of balls of ghostly fire seen rising from a swamp behind the house, which would then glide away. Some folks told stories of terrible vampires that haunted the grounds. Others had seen a witch in the area that would sweep you up on her broom and fly away with you.

Up the hollow behind the cabin was an old cave where Native American bones had been found. Reportedly, explorers also discovered giant and pygmy skeletons in this strange cave. Some folks told tales of pygmies dancing around the cave during thunderstorms. The strange beings waved sticks which caused the thunder to roar and lightning to brighten the sky (Kent 1955:102-105; 85-88).

Black Dog Road

Most of the roads in the Saltville area were packed down with cinders from the factory. The roads became black and dusty with the wagon and horse traffic. Travelers reported hearing footsteps behind them on some area roads and seeing dust clouds, but neither wagons nor horses would be visible. Many reports centered on a black dog and terrifying encounters along the roads. The dog would keep pace with the scared traveler and slide along through creeks, fences, and ditches alongside the road. Other unfortunate souls reported that the dog jumped up behind them as they rode their horses.

In 1900, a man named Tom Hurt reported a strange encounter with the black dog. As Tom was returning home from working late at the Mathieson screening plant, he saw the black dog appear. The dog followed him for almost a quarter of a mile, until Tom decided to test its mettle. He threw several large rocks, aiming at the white mark on the dog's head, but the rocks seemed to pass through and leave the dog unhurt. Tom then shot five lead balls into the dog; again, the dog didn't act hurt at all. At this point, Tom decided he had to destroy the dog. When they neared British Row, the dog ran ahead and disappeared at a large bridge on the road. Suddenly, Tom's hair raised, as he heard the panicked screams of woman coming from that area. Worrying that someone else had encountered the dog, he found a neighbor from a nearby house to help search for the woman. But, even with lanterns, they were unable to find a sign of the woman or the dog. Residents have seen this ghostly black dog many times lurking in the areas of Poor Valley from Tumbling Creek to Watson Gap and from Cedar Branch to Saltville. The mystery of the black dog remains unsolved (Kent 1955: 102-105; 85-88).

Musical Spooks on Country Roads

This story was included in a family history book of the Talbert family from Saltville. A man named Noah Talbert loved to play banjo at community parties and dances. Talbert cut quite a figure riding his big horse with his banjo hung across his back. Along one road in Saltville, an odd thing would happen. At night, when he passed a certain location on the road, he felt something climb on the horse's back behind him. Spooked, the horse would buck and kick and try to run away. Talbert looked over his shoulder and could see nothing. However, he could hear strumming as this spirit played his banjo. Talbert was never able to figure out who or what it was, but it seemed to enjoy banjo music (Harrington).

Saltville Witch

Also included in the book of Talbert family stories is a story told by Georgia Talbert Frazier, who grew up in Saltville. Once a man came to Molly's house to ask if she could draw an accurate picture of a witch named Cindy Holt. Folks believed this witch could put spells on people and animals, so the community feared her. The man planned to melt down enough silver dimes to make a silver bullet to shoot the drawing of the witch. Folks commonly believed that injuring a representation of a witch could harm her. Molly agreed to do the drawing but warned the man to never tell who had drawn the picture. The man promised to never tell of her identity. So, Molly drew a good representation of the witch Cindy Holt and gave it to the man. The man melted down his dimes to make a silver bullet and then shot the picture. He was happy that the bullet hit the picture, even though it barely grazed the witch's forehead.

Nobody had seen the witch in town for a long time. But, when she trudged down from the mountains, many noticed that she had a scar across her forehead in the spot that the bullet had grazed. The witch told folks she had fallen over a tree root in the woods and merely cut her forehead. The witch had a mission, though. She went right over to Molly's house and called her outside. Shaking with fear, Molly came out to face her. The witch said, "Molly, the next time you draw my picture, don't forget to put the band on my bonnet" (Harrington).

Yankees Get Peppered in Saltville

Years later, stories of the terror and devastation left by Union troops in raids through southwestern Virginia still linger. Saltville was the target for the Yankees raids, because of its precious supply of salt, which supplied the Confederate army and the region. In 1864, General Stephen Burbridge led the Yankees into Saltville to destroy the Preston Salt Works. The local people took their livestock, foods, and crowded the roads as they went into the mountains for protection.

One elderly lady lived near Saltville, but stayed in her house as the Yankees approached. She was boiling some brine in a large old black kettle in order to settle out the salt. People unfamiliar with the practice wouldn't know of the local method to extract salt for home use. One of the Union soldiers stopped, tipped his hat, and asked, "Grandmother, what is it that you're doing?" The tough old lady stood back, hands on her hips and squinted over to the group of Yankees on the road, and said "I'm a boilin' down brine for salt. But, you're not a-goin' to git salt, but peppered instead." The old lady was right! Although the federal troops numbered 5000 and the Confederates had only 3000 soldiers, the Yankees were defeated soundly at Sanders Hill in September 1864. General Burbridge led his "bullet peppered" troops back into Kentucky, leaving their wounded and dead behind (Angle, 2004; Kent 1991: 30-38).

Smyth County Civil War Heroine

During the Civil War, General Stoneman's raid through southwest Virginia struck fear in the residents' hearts. General Stoneman was on a mission to destroy the rail lines from Bristol up the Shenandoah Valley and cut off the salt supplies at Saltville for the Confederate Army and the region. In 1864, the residents of the area near Marion in Smyth County heard of Stoneman's approach and struggled to hide food, cattle, horses, and money from possible theft by the Yankees.

The Clerk of Smyth County in particular was fearful because he had heard of the fires set in Abingdon and it was his responsibility to preserve the country records. The clever clerk hid all the records in a wagon under some cotton goods and was ready to head for the near-by mountains. However, the Union army arrived and, for sport, set fire to the wagon and chased the clerk away. Legend has it that one of the Yankees approached an adjacent house and asked for a drink of water. In fear of retribution, a young daughter of the house polite-ly obliged. The soldier then told her that he knew calico was in short supply in the south and that if she wanted to she might have some from the burning wagon. She pretended an interest in finding the cloth and gave a charming curtsy. After the Yankees rode off, the 14 year-old girl put out the fire in the wagon and saved the county records. Later, Smyth County rewarded her $400 in Confederate money for her bravery (Angle, 2004).

Spells at the Coverston/Harris House

I included this story from Carol and Dave Schwartz about the Coverston/Harris house in Saltville because it aroused such curiosity and was a unique discovery in this region. The Museum of the Middle Appalachians in Saltville has featured an exhibit of the strange findings at the house.

Built in 1904, this historic house is located on Main Street in Saltville. The house is one of the Mathieson Alkali Works factory houses, all built about the same time in the early 1900s. Thomas T. Mathieson was from England, and he brought a number of workers from his home country, when he built the alkali plant in Saltville in 1893. This row of factory houses was built to house the workers, and the area was called "British Row." The first occupant of this particu-lar house was Prince Coverston, who was the head carpenter for Mathieson Alkaline. Coverston may have helped build the house himself.

Coverston/Harris house built 1904

The house has suffered extensive water damage and was being extensively renovated by Carol and Dave Schwartz. One of the construction workers telephoned Ms. Schwartz because he found some strange items between the lathe and the exterior walls. Ms. Schwartz returned to the house, and the builder showed her the odd assortment of items. The items had been carefully placed in between the walls and included: worn leather shoes (male, female, child, and infant), jacket, corset, suspenders, gloves, bow tie, umbrella, shoe polish tins, broken glass which seemed to be from a bowl, a wooden bottle with a cork, and a small stick shaped like a divining rod. Another interesting find were three glass bottles sealed with corks, one marked "poison." Also included within the walls were a collection of papers, including letters, (dating to the early 1900s) invoices, pencils, seed catalogs, and hypodermic needles. Neither the construction worker nor Carol had seen anything like this before. Everyone was confused over this find. Was this construction trash from the original construction of the house or was it something more?

Carol and Dave Schwartz were determined to solve this mystery. So, they've researched and found evidence to support a fascinating story explaining the concealed clothing and items. Since these houses were built to house British workers, it is likely they brought their own traditions over from their homeland. The explanation goes something like this: in England there has long been a tradition of concealing clothing, shoes, and personal items in the walls near entries, chimney flues, and windows to the house to keep evil spirits and witches away. The practice probably has its roots as far back as Roman times, when small animals or even babies were sacrificed and buried at the site of a new house to ward off evil. The concealed clothing superstition is based on the belief that evil spirits or witches will think the items are a person and can not enter the house.

The British commonly included worn shoes in this "spell" against evil, since they take on the shape of the wearer. Also, because of the accumulated sweat in shoes, they actually hold a part of you in them and may have magical properties. According to several Internet sites the Schwartzs consulted, bottles filled with poison, urine or pins, as well as broken glass, when concealed near an entry are believed to keep witches away from your house.

It's fascinating that the Schwartzs found these concealed objects in a Saltville house built for British workers. Similar caches have been discovered in California, New England, Florida and places were recent immigrants lived and brought with them their old world traditions. However, it's rare to find such a practice in southwestern Virginia, where most of the settlers were descendents from earlier European immigrants. For more information on this practice, consult the following web sites: www.concealedgarments.org (University of Southampton) or www.folkmagic.co.uk.

Carol and Dave Schwartz are enjoying renovating the house and restoring an important part of Saltville's history. Carol is originally from Saltville, so she feels as if she's coming home. In fact, she tells of entering the house and immediately experiencing a feeling of belonging and connection. The house may contain even more secrets, because Carol has seen a presence in the house. She saw a dark haired woman who smiled at her. When Carol blinked, the lady was gone. She and others have noticed an upstairs bedroom that has a warm feeling of a presence inside. This spirit seems to welcome them to the house, and Carol is not afraid of being alone there (Schwartz, 2004).

Ch. 11 Loud Ghosts in Goose Pimple Junction

Goose Pimple Junction is the unlikely name for a community located on Jonesboro Road and Junction Drive. This small crossroads community was once quite a busy place. The name of the community comes from an incident involving a family feud in the area. An elderly couple would wake folks up in the neighborhood when they started fighting and yelling each morning. L.B. Neese lived across from the family and decided that the place should be called Goose Pimple Junction because he got goose pimples every time the couple started "hollarin'" at each other. The old house was empty for many years after the couple passed away. Many say you can still see the old lady sitting on a rocker on the front porch and that you can hear the old man yelling at her from inside the house. Everyone in the community is afraid to walk by the old house after dark, especially on nights of the full moon.

In 1948, Annie and Bill Morrell put up a sign at the crossroads that proclaimed, "Goose Pimple Junction" and adjusted the population number. The old house is long gone as are the caretakers of the sign, but the memory of the place name remains (Cruise, 2004).

Final Words

I hope you've enjoyed reading these ghost stories, strange tales, and legends of Abingdon and Washington County. I learned many new things about the place I grew up by doing this research. For example, I was surprised to find so many Civil War stories, stories of conflicts with Native Americans, and stories of hidden treasure.

These stories are part of our Appalachian heritage and need to be preserved and retold to our children. It doesn't matter whether they're true or not, because they bring enjoyment to the audience. I have concluded that Abingdon and Washington County certainly have more than our fair share of ghosts, as well as old stories, and I hope they will live on. I will be working on a Volume 2 in this series in the future.

Sources

Aird, Brandon. "The Dark Side of Emory & Henry," Class Project for Diane Silver, Emory and Henry College, 2003.

Angle, L.C. Interview, 2004.

_____. "Oral History," 1996. Filed at Historical Society of Washington County, Virginia.

Angle L.C., Mary Joe Craig, Rhonda Craig, Walter Hendricks, R.C. Minton, Milton Smith. "Oral Histories." Filed at the Historical Society of Washington County, Virginia.

Aronhime, Gordon. "Holston Country During the Revolution: Not Really Quiet," *Bristol Herald Courier*, October 27, 1963.

_____. "One-Time Thriving Region Reverted to Wilderness After Indian Attack," *Bristol Herald Courier*, February 10, 1980.

_____. "Only Major Indian Battle of Area Holds Significant Place in History," *Bristol Herald Courier*, August 17, 1980.

_____. "Town House at Chilhowie," *Bristol Herald Courier*, March 31, 1963.

_____. "Woman, Child Hid as Indians Staged Raid," *Bristol Herald Courier*, March 10, 1963.

Barden, Thomas E., ed. *Virginia Folk Legends*, Charlottesville, VA: University Press of Virginia, 1991.

Bartlett, Charles S. Jr. and Lyle Browning. "Black's Fort Abingdon, Virginia Trial Excavation," 1998.

Brown, Pat. Interview, 2004.

Cole, Mattie Frazier. *A Story of the Settling and Growth of Chilhowie*. Tucker Printing, 1993.

Coletti, Vivian. Interview, 2004.

Crabtree, Lou. Interview, 2003.

Cruise, Donna. Interview, 2004.

Curtis, Claude D. *Three Quarters of a Century at Martha Washington College*. Bristol, TN/VA: King Printing Co., 1928

DeHart, Jennifer. Interview, 2004.

Glanville, Jim. "Conquistadors at Saltville in 1567? A Review of the Archeological and Documentary Evidence," *The Smithfield Review*, (Volume VIII, 2004) pp.70-108.

Gregory, Shannon. Interview, 2004.

Harrington, Mary Lou Frazier. Contributed family stories in the Talbert Family Book.

Hearl. G. Lee. Appalachian storyteller. Interview, 2004.

Henley, Helen, Matt, and Michael. Interview, 2004.

Historical Society of Washington County, Virginia. "A Self-Guided Tour of Sinking Spring Cemetery," filed at Historical Society of Washington County, Virginia.

Historical Society of Washington County, *Virginia Bulletin.* "Cultural Agencies of Southwest Virginia," by Dr. J.N. Hillman, (Bulletin #6).

Historical Society of Washington County, *Virginia Bulletin.* "Tales Told by Walls of House-Retirement," by Mary F. Landrum, (Series II, No 41), 2004.

Historical Society of Washington County, Virginia, Education Committee. "Washington County, VA Our Historic Home."

Historical Society of Washington County, Virginia Publication, "Historical Houses of Washington County, Virginia, (Series II, No. 6), Spring 1968.

Huff, B.B. Interview, 2004.

Hughes, Robert M. Annals and Reminiscences of an Octogenarian Feb. 19, 1936. On file at Historical Society of Washington County, Virginia.

Johnson, Dave and Jo. Interview, 2004.

Johnston Memorial Hospital staff members, Interviews 2004.

Kent, William B. *A History of Saltville.* 1955, reprint 1991.

King, Nanci. *Places in Time Vol. 1 Abingdon, Virginia 1778-1880.* 1989, second printing 1996.

King, Nanci. *Places in Time Vol. II Abingdon, Meadowview and Glade Spring, Virginia.* 1994.

King, Nanci. *Places in Time Vol. III, South from Abingdon to the Holston.* 1997.

Leidig, Dan. Interview, 2003.

Levenson, Phoebe. "House Near Glade Spring Was Built Century Ago in Era Just Before War," *The Roanoke Times,* December 28, 1958.

_____. "Washington Springs Paid An Unfair Price to Time," *Bristol Herald Courier,* 1959 (date unknown)

_____. "Area Home Has Colorful History," *Bristol Herald Courier,* March 15, 1959.

_____. "Old Plantation's History Recounts Long Series of Property Owners," *Bristol Herald Courier*, July 19, 1959.

_____. "Ancient Inn Recalls Days of Slaves, Stagecoaches," *Bristol Herald Courier*, August 9, 1959.

Litton, Glenn. Interview, 2003.

McConnell Catherine S. "Black's Fort," *Abingdon, Virginian*. August 2, 1978.

McGuinn, Doug. *The Virginia Creeper*. Boone, North Carolina, 1998.

McKinney, Bob. Interview, 2004.

Neal, J.Allen. *Bicentennial History of Washington County, Virginia 1776-1976*. Dallas, TX: Taylor Publishing Company, 1977.

Price, Charles Edwin. *The Mystery of Ghostly Vera and other Haunting Tales of Southwest Virginia*. Johnson City, TN: The Overmountain Press, 1993.

Salyers, Cynthia and Rob Salyers. Interview, 2004.

Schwartz, Carol. Interview, 2004.

Sensing, Thurman. *Champ Ferguson Confederate Guerilla*. Nashville, TN: Vanderbilt University Press, 1942.

Sexton, Scott. Interview, 2004.

Sheffey, Pete. Interview, 2003.

Stevenson, George J. *Increase in Excellence A History of Emory and Henry College*. New York: Meredith Publishing, 1963.

Summers, Lewis Preston. *History of Southwest Virginia 1746-1786 Washington County 1777-1870*. Johnson City, TN: The Overmountain Press, 1903, reprint 1989.

Sykes, Katie. "Haunted Emory," Class Project for Diane Silver at Emory and Henry College, 2003.

Taylor, L.B. *Ghosts of Virginia Vol. VI*. Progress Printing, 2001.

Vestal, Stanley. *Joe Meek The Merry Mountain Man*. Lincoln, NE: University of Nebraska Press, 1952.

Victor, Frances Fuller. *The River of the West: The Adventures of Joe Meek*. Missoula: Mountain Press Publishing Company, 1870, reprint 1983.

Virginia Department of Historic Landmarks Historic (VDHL) District/Brief Survey 95-04, "Brook Hall," Vivian Coletti, 1993.

VDHL District/Brief Survey 95-0010, "Kilmakronen," Vivian Coletti, 1993.

VDHL District/Brief Survey 95-26, "Kirk-Meek House," Vivian Coletti, 1993.

VDHL District/Brief Survey 95-48, "Indian Fields," Vivian Coletti, 1993.

VDHL District /Brief Survey 95-135, "Old Glade Church/Ebbing Springs," Vivian Coletti, 1993.

VDHL District/Brief Survey 95-218, "Blacksburg," Vivian Coletti, 1993.

VDHL District/Brief Survey 95-277 "Ebbing Springs Meeting House," Vivian Coletti, 1993.

VDHL District/Brief Survey 95-436, "Byars House," Vivian Coletti, 1993.

VDHL District/Brief Survey 95-0443, "Beattie House," Vivian Coletti, 1993.

VDHL District/Brief Survey 95-0468, "Smith Tavern," Vivian Coletti, 1993.

VDHL Historic District/Brief Survey 95-501, "McConnell House," Vivian Coletti, 1993.

Weisfeld, Robert. Interview, 2003.

Williams, Eleanor. Interview, 2003.

Williams, Stan. "Glade Spring," Published by the Historical Society of Washington County, Virginia, 1998.

Williams, Stan and Jennifer Wagner. "Meadowview," Published by the Historical Society of Washington County, Virginia, 1998.

Willis, Jason. "Shadows of the Imagination: The Ghosts of Emory," Class project for Diane Silver at Emory and Henry College, 2003.

Wilson, Goodridge A. "Meek House Was Center of Stirring Times in Southwest," *The Roanoke Times*, January 24, 1932.

_____. *Smyth County History and Traditions.* Kingsport, TN: Kingsport Press. 1932.

About the Author — Donna Akers Warmuth

Donna enjoys making local history come alive for the average person who's not interested in reading a thick history book. Her first book, *Plumb Full of History A Story of Abingdon, Virginia,* received excellent reviews from Lee Smith and Sharyn McCrumb. She has also compiled three books in the Images of America series: *Boone, Blowing Rock,* and *Abingdon Virginia,* collections of 200 historic photographs and postcards of the communities. Her next book is an Images of America book on Washington County, Virginia which will be available in 2006.

Donna's stories, articles, and poetry have been published in *Appalachian Heritage, Branches and Smoky Mountain Living.* Her works have placed in contests held by *Now & Then* and the Virginia Highlands Festival Creative Writing program. She has also contributed essays to the Morning Edition on WNCW in Spindale, North Carolina. Her books have won awards from High Country Writers.

Donna lives with her husband, Greg, and two young sons, Owen and Riley, in Boone, North Carolina. Donna is available for school programs and presentations on local history, Appalachian heritage, in-service teacher training and writing workshops.

Contact her at:

Donna Akers Warmuth
410 Parkcrest Drive
Boone, NC 28607
(828) 268-0970
www.donnawarmuth.com

OTHER BOOKS BY DONNA AKERS WARMUTH

Plumb Full of History A Story of Abingdon, Virginia
2002, High Country Publishers
ISBN 1-932158-78-2
$9.95

    This story of two children discovering much more than the history of their grandmother's hometown will be enjoyed by both youth and adults. Ghost stories, legends, and history all turn a stroll down Abingdon's Plumb Alley into an exciting and educational adventure.

Abingdon, Virginia: Images of America
2002, Arcadia Publishing
ISBN 0-7385-1489-6
$19.99

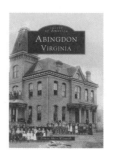

    This collection of historic photographs and postcards illustrates the distinct charm and beauty of historic Abingdon. Rare images with informative captions provide a glimpse into the past of this unique town.

Boone: Images of America
2003, Arcadia Publishing
ISBN 0-7385-1541-8
$19.99

    Explore the North Carolina town named for Daniel Boone. Originally called the Lost Provinces, Boone today is a thriving college town, arts center, and tourist destination. This book is a photographic journey through the history of this charming mountain town.

Blowing Rock: Images of America
2004, Arcadia Publishing
ISBN 0-7385-1647-3
$19.99

    Using archival photographs and postcards, this book presents the distinctive story of Blowing Rock. Catch a glimpse of small-town charm, friendly faces, and inspiring scenery that make the village a prime vacation destination.

Available through bookstores, major on-line book retailers, and through Donna Akers Warmuth's website: <u>www.donnawarmuth.com</u>

Look for upcoming books: Washington County, Virginia (Images of America), Volume 2 of Legends and Ghost Stories of Washington County, and a book on the Overmountain Men and their march.